LONDON GROWL

AN IAN DEX SUPERNATURAL THRILLER NOVEL, #4

JOHN P. LOGSDON
CHRISTOPHER P. YOUNG

CRIMSON MYTH
PRESS

Published by: Crimson Myth Press (www.CrimsonMyth.com)

Cover art: Jake Logsdon (www.JakeLogsdon.com)

Thanks to TEAM ASS!
Advanced Story Squad

This is the first line of readers of the series. Their job is to help me keep things in check and also to make sure I'm not doing anything way off base in the various story locations!

(listed in alphabetical order by first name)

Bennah Phelps
Cassandra Hall
Hal Bass
John Debnam
Larry Diaz Tushman
Marie McCraney
Mike Helas
Natalie Fallon
Noah Sturdevant
Paulette Kilgore
Penny Campbell-Myhill
Soobee Dewson

Thanks to Team DAMN
Demented And Magnificently Naughty

This crew is the second line of readers who get the final draft of the story, report any issues they find, and do their best to inflate my fragile ego.

(listed in alphabetical order by first name)

Adam Goldstein, Adam Saunders-Pederick, Amanda Holden, Amy Robertson, Andrew Greeson, Angie Hill, Bennah Phelps, Bob Topping, Bonnie Dale Keck, Brandy Dalton, Carla Wagner, Carolyn Fielding, Carolyn Jean Evans, Cassandra Hall, Charlotte Webby, David Botell, Debbie Tily, Denise King, Helen Day, Ian Nick Tarry, Jacky Oxley, Jamie Gray, Jan Gray, Jim Stoltz, Jo Dungey, Jodie Stackowiak, John Debnam, Kate Smith, Kathleen Portig, Kathryne Nield, Kevin Frost, Koren Small, Larry Diaz Tushman, Laura Maria Redmond, Laura Stoddart, Lucas Warwick, Mark Beech, Mark Brown, Mark Junk, Mary Geren, MaryAnn Sims, Megan McBrien, Megan Thigpen, Mike Helas, Myles Mary Cohen, Natalie Fallon, Noah Sturdevant, Pam Junkins, Paulette Kilgore, Pete Sandry, Ruth Nield, Sandee Lloyd, Scott Reid, Stephen Bagwell, Tammy Tushman, Tehrene Hart.

CHAPTER 1

*T*he guy cut down into the west parking garage of the Palms faster than anyone I'd ever chased before.

To be fair, he was a djinn.

And a naughty one at that.

During my years in the Las Vegas Paranormal Police Department, I had learned a thing or two about the complexities of dealing with various supernatural races. Vampires were at the top on the scale of pains in the ass because they believed they were better than everyone else. Werewolves came in second, not because they thought themselves better, but because when they slipped into full wolf form they tended to forget that they weren't supposed to eat people. Mages were next. Power corrupts, you know.

Djinn, however, had a tendency to be somewhat easygoing. At least that was true in the Overworld. This was because they were paid quite well to provide mental excursions to wealthy customers. That meant they were in demand. It also meant that they didn't have to resort to fear tactics, forced-comas, and all the other fun things that they tended to be capable of inflicting on folks.

This guy, however, was being a real dick.

It seemed that there had been a Netherworld prison break a few days back. A flurry of escapees flooded the Netherworld areas, bringing their PPD to their knees as they worked to corral everyone before too many people got hurt.

But some of them got topside.

That meant we had to deal with them along with Retriever units. These weren't canines, and I'd learned the hard way that you didn't want to refer to them as that. They really didn't like it. Retrievers were cops who didn't quite fit in with the rest of the crowd. Doing standard police work for them was like sitting in a dentist's chair and having a root canal—without pain killers. But Retrievers also tended to be those who could possibly end up in a life of crime were there no better alternatives. They were thrill-seekers, rebellious types, who were often outcasts or badasses. They also tended to be entrepreneurially minded. While they collected a standard paycheck, like any cop, they were paid much less. This was because they were paid commissions for every perp that got brought back alive. Kind of like bounty hunters, who were also on payroll. Before the PPD went with this method of payment, very few perps made it back alive.

The djinn we were chasing was one of the escaped from the Netherworld. That put us in a bad spot in three ways. First, he had nothing to lose but his freedom, meaning he was more than willing to cause as much damage as he could in order to avoid going back to prison. Second, we couldn't just outright kill him unless he was killing people in our city, which he wouldn't do because he knew that would give us carte blanche to knock his ass out. Third, while we had to keep the guy busy, we knew full well that it was only a matter of time before a Retriever team showed up to claim him.

Fun.

It was at times like these that I wished Rachel Cress, my partner of seven years, was still by my side. But she'd left after our last battle against an ubernatural, claiming it was too painful to work side by side with me anymore. This was because we used to be an item...before I'd become the chief of the Vegas PPD.

For now, I had Harvey as my partner. He was a werebear who was new to the force. We'd brought him in because he'd helped us fight against a nutty necromancer a number of months back. He wasn't exactly cop material. At least not in the traditional sense. In his mind, being a cop was doing stuff like cops did in old TV shows. Currently he was wearing a cowboy hat, but I wasn't sure which show that was supposed to represent. Anyway, he was a good guy and his heart was in the right place. He just needed time to get the hang of things.

"Harvey," I said, "you have to keep your gun at the ready."

"Right," he replied as we continued chasing after the djinn. "I keep forgetting. I'm used to just turning into a bear when threatened."

I gave him a sidelong glance. "Which would go over swell in a casino full of normals."

"Can't see how a six-foot-five guy running around with a .50 caliber Desert Eagle is much better."

The fact was that every weapon used by PPD officers was imbued with its own null zone. This made it so people didn't freak out about the fact that we were carrying weapons. The null zones rendered them effectively invisible. Some cops asked for them to have particular visuals when mortals saw them, like a flashlight or something. I'd considered having Boomy made to look like a dildo, but that probably would have been worse than people just seeing a gun. I did laugh pretty heartily at the thought of someone yelling, "Look out, he's got a dildo!"

Still, he had a point.

"Fair enough," I admitted and pointed ahead. "Looks like Tats is heading up the elevator."

"Tats?"

"He's covered with tattoos," I explained an instant before we burst through the doors to the stairs.

There were already a few twitching bodies on the ground as we ran through the main casino floor. He was heading straight toward Garduño's, which used to be Hooters. This day would have been a whole lot better if it still was Hooters. Not that I had anything against Garduño's. In fact, I rather liked it. But...*Hooters*!

"Lydia," I called through the connector to our A.I. dispatch back at base, "I need you to inform The Spin that we've got a bunch of bodies on the ground here."

"Dead, sweetie?" she replied with a voice of concern.

"No, just in la-la land, having either the best fantasies of their lives or the worst nightmares."

"We've got bodies over at the Bellagio, too," Jasmine chimed in. "Serena's going to be working overtime clearing all these heads."

"She'll need help," I noted. "Have her get in touch with the head of the Djinn Ink Club and work a deal. They'll do what they can since they don't want any trouble."

"You got it, puddin'," Lydia replied, always one to flirt with me. "And just so you know, in addition to Jasmine's report, I'm also getting reports from all the officers about masses of bodies in the various casinos."

"Paula ought to have a field day with this," I stated, almost wanting to laugh but knowing better. I wasn't worried she could hear me or anything, but seeing that she was one of my ex-girlfriends, the thought of doing or saying anything that could even potentially cause a karmic shift in the universe that resulted in pouring her wrath in my direction wasn't worth it. "Let her know we'll help however we can, once we get everything under control."

We wouldn't. We never did. But it'd appease Paula to hear that we *would* help, if asked.

Lydia acknowledged just as Tats hit the elevator and headed down to the east garage.

"Why do I have the feeling that this fucker is just running us in circles?" I said aloud.

"Looks like he might be," agreed Harvey, who was panting from the run. "Want me to go back the other way?"

"No," I replied. "You keep on his tail and I'll circle back.

I have the feeling he's having way too much fun with this little game, so one more round is quite likely." I grabbed Harvey by the arm. "Keep your gun at the ready and only shoot him in the leg or something."

"Got it."

"And, Harvey," I yelled back as we broke apart, *"don't* let him touch you."

CHAPTER 2

I got back to the west garage and turned on the jets to get to the entrance.

Sure enough, Tats was there.

Fortunately, he hadn't seen me.

He was pressed against the wall with a creepy grin on his face. Obviously he had something planned. What that was, I couldn't say, but seeing as how he was really enjoying his small window of freedom, it couldn't be good.

I moved slowly with Boomy at the ready. Technically, we weren't supposed to kill the guy, but my finger was feeling pretty itchy. If I channeled what I'm certain Paula Rose was going to be feeling about having to clean up the mess Tats was making, I'd have busted multiple caps in his ass already.

One thing I *could* do was target his shins or feet. It wouldn't kill him, but it'd sure make his running a lot slower. Plus, the pain he'd feel would make me a whole lot happier.

I just had to get closer to do it, since all I could see was his upper body. There were too many cars in the way.

Just as I was getting in range, Harvey turned the corner and ran right into him.

Tats smiled even bigger as he reached out and put his hand on Harvey's shoulder.

Shit.

Harvey's eyes rolled up into his head, but he stayed standing.

I knew Tats was planning something naughty.

As if in response to that thought, Tats turned and looked right at me. He'd obviously known I was creeping up on him because he wore a face of joyful menace.

He winked.

This *really* wasn't good.

Harvey shook for a couple of seconds and then went deathly still.

Tats removed his hand from the werebear's shoulder and then turned to me and crossed his arms in smug defiance.

My new partner opened his eyes and stared into mine. It was a cold stare. It was one of those stares that made you think you were about to get hurt.

I gulped.

Most of the officers on my squad were deadly. It was part of the gig, after all. But there was something about a werebear, in human form or not, that chilled you to the core. They were fierce, huge, and deadly. Yeah, I was an amalgamite, so I had the ability to do a lot of different things, and I was pretty strong, agile, and fast, but going head to head with Harvey in a death match wasn't exactly what I'd call fun. If he got hold of me, it'd hurt. It may even be one of those hurts that I wouldn't come back from.

At the same time, it wasn't like I could just shoot him. Well, I *could*, but I wouldn't feel great about it. He was a fellow officer. And he wasn't himself. Tats had clearly done something to mess with his mind….it's what djinns did. I also wasn't going to pull the old "Harvey, are you in there?" bullshit in the hopes that he'd fight against his mental imprisonment and not cause me any grave discomfort. It wouldn't work. That's just stuff they did in movies to solve a difficult plot point.

So, I ran.

I was almost hoping Harvey was going to turn into a werebear, but he just yelled and came running after me.

That was good and bad.

It was good because I'd be able to cut a corner and knock his ass out. It was bad because if I failed to knock his ass out, he'd knock my ass out…or worse.

I cut behind a van and slipped along the wall as the sound of his pounding feet slowed. He wasn't going to be able to smell me as well in his current form, especially since the area stank of gas fumes.

But something told me it wasn't just Harvey's brain doing the work here. Tats had to have some connection going on.

I dropped to the ground and scanned under the cars. Harvey was pacing along slowly, hunting his prey.

He stopped.

I held my breath.

His shoes angled away slightly and then his hands hit the ground. A second later I saw his eyes locking on to mine. Those eyes did *not* belong to the Harvey I knew. Well, I mean, technically they did, but the life currently behind them was owned by a madman.

Okay, so I wasn't dealing with Harvey, and that meant I had no choice but to fight this guy like he was Tats.

With a sigh, I pushed myself up and put Boomy back in his holster.

Then I stepped out.

"Okay, pal," I said as I cracked my neck from side to side, "you obviously want this to be fun, so let's have some fun."

"I'm listening," said Harvey's voice, though it clearly wasn't Harvey's inflection.

"Let's go hand to hand on this. No weapons, no mental games, just fists, feet, and grappling."

Harvey nodded slowly.

"While that *does* sound interesting," Tats-through-Harvey said, "I think I'll just shoot you."

My partner's hand came up and his Desert Eagle pointed right at me.

"Harvey," I said hopefully, "are you in there?"

CHAPTER 3

I dropped straight to the ground as the first bullet flew overhead. Then I rolled behind a car as the second one bounced off the ground next to me.

It was desperation time.

I yanked Boomy free, peered around the tire I was nestled behind, and shot Harvey in the shin.

He screamed and fell forward as I got up and ran right at him. It only took me a couple of seconds to get there, but it wouldn't have mattered anyway seeing that he was writhing around in pain.

"What the hell did you shoot me for, boss?" he asked through gritted teeth.

"Because you were trying to kill me, Harvey," I replied calmly. "Well, *you* weren't, but Tats had gotten control of your mind and was using you to take me out."

"I don't remember any of that," he said, still groaning.

"Do you remember how you got over here?"

He looked around through his wince. "No."

"Exactly." I put a call in to Lydia and told her to get a medic down here right away. "Stay put," I commanded. "I'm going to get that fucker."

"Wait," he said, grabbing my leg. "I can sense him."

"What?"

"It's weird. I guess when he was controlling me, like you said, he somehow either left the channel open or it doesn't break that easily." He went to stand up and then clearly remembered that he had a hole in his shin. "Shit! Fuck! Tits! Balls! Ass!"

I knew that feeling.

"Where is he?" I said, trying to get Harvey to focus back on Tats. "I know this hurts, but I've got to stop this guy."

"I know, I know," Harvey replied through ragged breaths. "He's..." His eyes opened and he looked right at me. Then he whispered, "He's waiting for you."

"Where?" I mouthed.

He pointed and curved his hand to let me know that the djinn was right around the corner.

So he was going to try and control me like he had Harvey? Well, we'd just have to see about that. This guy had just moved into deadly mode, meaning that I had the right to kill him.

Just in case, I snatched up Harvey's Eagle and stuck it in Boomy's holster. I had no desire to find out that this was just some kind of ruse to get me to let my guard down so Tats could resume his control of Harvey and drop a few bullets in my back.

I moved like a cat until I was within range of the spot where Tats was supposedly hiding. Then I took a deep breath, pumped my adrenaline, and spun around the corner with Boomy held high.

Unfortunately, I was aiming too high.

Tats was crouched.

By the time I adjusted, Tats had reached out and grabbed my arm.

He didn't try to disarm me but rather was attempting to control me like he'd done to Harvey.

I didn't feel anything.

This wasn't surprising to me, but it was apparent that Tats found his lack of power disturbing at best.

"What the hell?" he rasped as he redoubled his grip, raised a determined eyebrow, and stared into my eyes.

Nothing.

"I don't understand," he said, confused. "Are you wearing some type of protection amulet or is there a spell on you?"

"No, dipshit," I replied, slapping his arm away and shoving him back against the wall. "I'm an amalgamite. Your crazy mind-crap doesn't work on me."

"A…what?"

"Look it up on the other side of life, pal," I said, placing Boomy against his head.

His eyes grew frantic. "Wait, wait."

"No, no."

"We'll take it from here, Officer Dex," came a voice that I'd not heard in a very long time. So long, in fact, that it took me a second to place it. "Lower your weapon…now."

I glanced over my shoulder to see two Retrievers standing there. I only knew one of them.

"Piper?" I asked.

"Yes," she replied.

Sure enough, it was Piper Shaw, Retriever extraordinaire.

I gave her the onceover. She looked good. Lithe with a short hairstyle that hadn't changed since the last time I saw her. It was dirty blond now, though. Piper still had that permanent look of determination on her face. Of course, that visage seemed to be a mainstay for Retrievers. It was best seen when bedding down with one, which I'd done with Piper many years ago.

Next to her was a thirty-something guy who was wearing a trench coat, a black, brimmed hat, and a goatee that led off to connect to sideburns in a tight line that ran along his jaw. He looked relatively normal, except for his glowing eyes.

"You look good," I said to Piper.

She looked me over. "Thanks. You, too."

"And this is?" I said, motioning to Mr. Glowy Eyes.

"Reaper," she said and then rolled her eyes. "Reaper Payne, this is Ian Dex."

"Ah," said Reaper in a voice that seemed rather calm. "You're the amalgamite."

"Yep," I replied with a nod. "And you're a...what, exactly?"

"Former reaper," he answered.

I blinked. "As in the dude who takes people into the afterlife?"

"One of them, yes," he replied. "There are many of us."

Talk about a demotion.

"So you're a reaper, but you work for the PPD as a Retriever?"

"Correct," he said as Piper went over and subdued Tats, who looked like he was more than willing to give up at this point. "I'm being punished for transgressions against my Order."

"Oh," I said and then shrugged. "Cool."

He held up a finger. "Please don't kill him, Piper."

"I said I wouldn't," she said.

"Thank you." Reaper then whispered to me, "We're paid on commission, you know? I have rent to pay."

"Ah."

Reaper suddenly glanced in the direction of Harvey. "I sense someone is injured."

"My partner is," I stated, holding up my hands. "*Injured*, not dead. Don't get any ideas, pal."

Reaper tilted his head at me as if confused.

"Don't be a dumbass, Ian," Piper said. "Reaper can heal the guy."

"Oh, sorry."

We walked over to Harvey and found he'd already passed out. Being shot wasn't much fun. Trust me; I knew.

Reaper knelt down and placed his hand on the wound. A glow emanated from him much like the light show that my mages used. It was clear that this guy had at least some level of magic flowing through his veins, which I guess made sense seeing what he was normally.

Harvey sat up straight and yelped, but Reaper held on to his leg and kept his focus.

"Chill out, Harvey," I said, putting my hand on his chest. "This guy is a reaper."

"What?" Harvey yelled, his face going white. "I'm not dead, right?"

I frowned at him. "Would I be standing here if you were?"

And they called *me* an idiot.

"You might have died too," Harvey shot back.

Valid point.

"Well, I'm not dead."

"Are you sure?" His brow was furrowed. "There *is* a reaper here, right?"

"Yes, I'm sure. He's a member of the PPD now. He works in the Retriever unit because he got in trouble with the Reaper Clan or something."

"Order," Reaper corrected. "Clan is a dirty word where I come from."

"Is here, too," I conceded. "Well, depending on context anyway."

Reaper stood back up and pulled Harvey to his feet.

Harvey tentatively put weight on his leg.

Then he smiled.

"Should be good as new," Reaper said without inflection.

Harvey slapped Mr. Glowy Eyes on the arm. "Feels great!"

Reaper merely nodded in response.

"All right," said Piper as she dragged Tats over to where we were standing. The djinn looked to be in a daze. "This was the last one. Thanks to the rest of your team. Blah blah blah."

"So heartfelt," I replied.

She pointed at me. "And if this ever happens again, see if you guys can be a little quicker about things, okay?"

I gave her my best duck look.

"How about you guys making sure this never happens again?" I countered with a grunt.

"Not my jurisdiction to stop prison breaks," she stated. "My job is to bring back lawbreakers."

"Right. Well, it was simply a pleasure seeing you again."

She nodded in an I-don't-believe-you sort of way.

Then she paused and gave me another onceover.

"Actually, we should get together sometime," she said with what was *almost* a smile. "It was fun last time."

"Fun?" I scoffed at that. "As I recall, you were using a whip last time we were together."

"Like I said," she replied mischievously, "it was fun."

"Right."

CHAPTER 4

After a quick check with all my officers, I headed up to meet with the Directors. This wasn't exactly the most enjoyable part of my job, but being the chief wasn't always glamorous.

"Sweetie," said Lydia before I walked into the meeting room that sat at the back of my office, "Paula Rose would like to speak with you."

"I'm about to go into—"

"She says it's urgent, puddin'."

"Fine," I said with a sigh. "Put her through to my connector, please."

"I have Officer Dex for you, Ms. Rose," Lydia said.

"Ian?"

"Yes, Paula?"

"What the fuck did you do this time?" Her voice was tight yet controlled. She wasn't screaming at me or anything. I hated it when she was like this. It meant that her level of irritation was far beyond the norm. "I've got bodies all over the damn place here!"

"Is the Ink Club helping?" I said, keeping myself calm.

"Well, yes, but—"

"Then what's the problem?"

"Do you have any idea how difficult this is going to be to spin?"

"Oh, come on, Paula," I said with a laugh. "You've got the Djinn Ink Club *right there* with you."

"So? If they…" She stopped. "Oh, wait." Another pause. "Oh, wow."

I smiled. "Exactly."

"I could get a commission on this, too," she said. "Assuming that djinn didn't throw people into nightmares. But even then, the Ink Club could fix that…right?"

"Yes."

"Oh, this is great!"

"See?" I stated as firmly as I could. "It's not *always* a negative thing when this stuff happens. And remember, nobody was killed."

"This time."

"Which means something, right?"

"Yeah," she replied. "I guess it does. Thanks, Ian. I owe you one."

Now *that* was rare.

"No problem," I answered. "I have to run to a meeting now."

We disconnected and I walked into the meeting with the Directors.

They were all waiting for me, but I couldn't really see

them. Well, I saw wisps of them mostly, though sometimes I'd catch a full visual. But it never lasted. It would fade from memory super fast. That's the way it was with these guys, though. It was meant as some form of protection for them, I suppose.

On the left was Silver, the head of the Vegas Vampires. Next was Zack, leader of the Vegas Werewolf pack. O was the mage who controlled the Crimson Focus Mages in Vegas. Finally, EQK ran the Vegas Pixies.

"Are we correct in understanding that everything is under control?" asked O.

"Yes, sir," I replied as I took my seat in front of them. I felt like I was giving testimony at a political investigation. "The Spin is currently working with the Djinn Ink Club to assuage fears, too. They're going to use this as a way of showing what kind of fun people can have if they visit the club."

"But won't that mean people will be exposed to the fact that the djinn are supernatural?" said Silver.

"I'm sure Paula will spin it in such a way as to make it seem like just a magic trick of some sort."

"Like hypnosis," Zack stated. "It's a good idea."

"Thank you, sir."

"Pixies can't be hypnotized, you know," EQK announced. "Our brains are far more advanced than your Neanderthal-like clumps of goop."

"Anyway, Mr. Dex," O said before EQK could get started on one of his insulting rampages, "we have some information for you that is going to be unsettling."

I didn't like the sound of that.

"Sir?" I said.

"Now, you must understand that we are with you one hundred percent here," O said before revealing the news.

"Thanks."

"And you must also know that—"

"Oh, for fuck's sake," EQK blurted, "you're slower than a snail with an erection."

I saw a flash of O as he leaned forward. "Excuse me?"

"You're excused," EQK said sincerely. "Dex, your ex-partner was kidnapped."

I stood up. "Rachel?"

"Do you have another ex-partner that we don't know about?" asked EQK with a smattering of sarcasm. "Of course it's Rachel, you walnut."

"Where is she?" I said, my pulse rising. "Has she been hurt?"

"London PPD says that they received a note that she was taken and that they would be given instructions in a few days as to what their demands are," explained Zack. "If the demands are met, she'll be released."

My mind was racing. I couldn't just sit idly by while Rachel was in trouble. Yes, she was the one who'd made the decision to leave the Vegas PPD and, yes, she said that she could no longer be around me...but she'd been my partner for seven years! She meant more to me than anyone I knew, and my team was like a family to me, so that was really saying something.

"I'm going," I said.

"We fully expected that," Silver replied. "We also know that the rest of your team will want to join you, but we obviously can't allow that. Therefore, you must choose who will be your replacement while you're gone."

"Officer Benchley," I answered without hesitation.

"Fine."

I made for the door.

"Mr. Dex," O said before I could leave, "please know that we are fully behind you, whatever you need to do here. We all understand what it means to have a partner in trouble."

"I don't," stated EQK.

Silver groaned. "You're a real asshole, EQK, you know that?"

"Thanks, Silver," EQK said genuinely. "That means a lot to me. I think you're an asshole, too."

Silver groaned again.

CHAPTER 5

*J*had Lydia call everyone to the meeting room. This was not going to be a fun one. I knew that everyone was going to want to join me on this mission, but it couldn't be done and they had to deal with that.

"Listen up," I said as they all sat down. "I just got word that Rachel has been kidnapped in London."

"What?" growled Felicia, her eyes going instantly red.

I put my hands up. "I know that all of you feel the same way I do about this, and I'm sure every one of you wants to go and help, but you have to realize that you must stay here and protect this city."

Their faces were ones of sheer determination. I got that. I felt it, too.

"Here's what's going to happen," I said before anyone could start to argue. "Griff is going to be in charge while I'm gone."

"Wait, you're going?" snapped Serena. "Why are you going and the rest of us have to stay?"

"Because Rachel was *my* partner, Serena." I'd said it more harshly than I probably should have. I took a breath. "Sorry. She was my partner. If we were talking about Chuck being kidnapped, Griff would be going. If it was Felicia who had been taken, Jasmine would be heading out the door." I looked from face to face. "That's not the case here. Rachel was the one taken and so I'm the one going."

Everyone looked irritated at this, but they also seemed to get the point.

"Again," I continued, "I'm leaving Griff in charge of the precinct while I'm gone." I turned to him. "Hopefully things will be standard run-of-the-mill stuff, but if anything bad turns up, just do whatever you think I'd do." Then I sighed. "Shit, you already know that. Hell, you're probably *still* more qualified than me to have this position, Griff."

"I will uphold the position faithfully," he said in his posh way. "I shall even attend to any meetings that the Directors wish to convene."

"Yeah," I said, shaking my head. "Good luck with that."

Chuck sat up. "Are you bringing any of us with you?"

"Harvey," I said, pointing at my partner. I'd just assumed he'd want to go, but the fact was that he was still a rookie. Putting him in this position this early in his career was probably a bit unfair. "Assuming you're okay with going, Harvey?"

"To London?" he asked with a huge grin. "Hell, yeah.

I've always wanted to go there. It's where Sherlock Holmes did all of his sleuthing, you know?"

I squeezed my eyebrows together. "Yeah, okay."

"Wait a second here," said Felicia. "No offense to Harvey, but he's still pretty green. He's got no idea how to—"

"I know what you're going to say, Felicia," I interrupted before she could instill fear into my new partner, "but Harvey's been doing just fine by my side over these last couple of months. We have a rapport and he knows what I expect from him." That wasn't really true at all. Frankly, Harvey was rather trying at times, but I needed to keep everyone else here doing their jobs. "Plus, I'm sure I'll be provided with one or two seasoned officers from the London PPD. They know more about their city than we do, right?"

Felicia looked away.

"Again, guys, I know how all of you feel about Rachel, but this is how it's going to be." I glanced at them all. "Are we clear?"

Like a bunch of school kids who were just told that they had to write a "What I did on my summer vacation" paper, they grumbled their reply.

"I promise to keep Lydia informed," I added, "and she'll keep everyone else up to date on what's happening."

Nobody said a word for the next few moments, though Harvey looked more excited than concerned.

He was nearly beaming.

I couldn't quite blame him since this was going to be an adventure, of sorts. From his perspective, anyway. The fact was that he didn't know Rachel all that well, so he wasn't as emotionally charged as the rest of the group.

"Right," I said finally. "Harvey and I are going to head out now. Griff, keep everyone in line while I'm gone."

"I shall."

"Good luck, Chief," said Chuck.

"Yeah," agreed the rest of the crew.

"You have enough ammo?" asked Turbo before I turned toward the door. "I can line your jackets, if you want?"

"Actually," I said, checking my reserves, "that would be good. Line Harvey's too, please?"

Turbo flew like a shot from the room, calling, "You got it," over his shoulder.

The crew split up and Harvey and I headed to my office.

"Lydia," I said aloud, "please hook us up with a direct portal to the London PPD precinct where Rachel works."

"You'll have to go through the Netherworld system, honey," she explained. "It's just a brief jump point, though. Shouldn't take but a few minutes."

"Fine," I said with a sigh.

"Turbo said that he has your ammunition ready," Lydia stated. "Promise me you'll be careful, puddin'?"

"I'll try, Lydia," I answered. "I'll try."

Harvey grimaced and looked up at the ceiling.

"I'm going too, Lydia," he said, sounding hurt. "Don't you care if I'm going to be careful or not?"

"Actually, Harvey," Lydia said slightly less pedantically than she sounded with the other officers, "I *do* hope you're careful, too. I think you're humorous."

"Yeah?" he said, all smiles. "Thanks, Lydia. I think you're a lot of fun, too."

"Really?"

"Heck yeah. You're much cooler than Siri, I can tell you that!"

"Aw shucks," Lydia said with a digital giggle. "You're too kind."

CHAPTER 6

$\mathcal{W}$e reached the Netherworld portal at the main PPD station house. This was where all officers started their processing and training.

You'd think it would be some incredible digital world with floating screens and cops all dressed in plain suits. It wasn't. It was a lot more like the regular police stations you saw in the Overworld. There were desks all over the place, and they were covered in paperwork and coffee stains. Regular cops wore standard green outfits, detectives had on the shirt and tie, but nothing that marked them as fashionistas. The Retrievers all went with that Piper and Reaper look, meaning they wore trench coats, hats, and anything else you could think of that fit the clandestine visual.

The place was bouncing with activity. Djinn were being processed everywhere.

I tried to seek out the one who had been messing with me and Harvey, but being covered from head to toe with tattoos made everyone look pretty similar to each other. I was sure if I could catch a direct glance into his eyes, I'd recognize him, but it wasn't worth the effort. Piper had nabbed him, so he'd be back in jail in no time.

"This place is great," Harvey said in a voice of awe. "It looks like an episode of *Barney Miller*, but with a lot more desks."

I wasn't familiar with the show. I just shrugged and turned my attention back to the portal so we could get ourselves to London.

"Lydia," I said through the connector, knowing that relays would allow me to fully communicate with her, "do you know the code for getting me into the London PPD from here?"

"Seven-seven-three-nine-four," she replied. "Just so you know, honeycakes, that won't take you directly to the precinct. It will drop you at St. Martin-in-the-Fields."

"We're going to be in the middle of a field?" I asked while entering in the code.

"It's a church, silly," she giggled. "You'll end up in a null zone near the exit. Nobody will notice you."

"Got it," I said, but I hesitated again. "So where is their PPD?"

"It's in the National Gallery, across the way from the church."

"Walking distance?"

"Yes."

"Thanks, baby," I said.

Just as I was about to hit the button, I looked over and saw that Harvey was not standing with me. A quick scan put him about halfway down the row of desks. He was talking with someone I couldn't see.

"Damn it," I said as I strode after him.

When I got there, I saw he was speaking with Reaper.

"Hey, Chief," Harvey said excitedly. "I was just thanking Reaper here for fixing my leg earlier. Worked like a charm, you know?"

"Officer Dex," Reaper said with a nod.

"Reaper," I replied in kind. "Sorry for the interruption."

"It's not a problem. I rarely have the opportunity to speak with people who live topside. Well, at least not people who are living there legally. When I was still in the Order, I was only able to speak with them after they'd expired."

"Ah," I said, checking my watch. "Well, you should come up for a beer sometime, then."

He inclined his head. "That would be nice."

"Cool. Harvey, we have to go. Rachel, remember?"

"Are you speaking of Rachel Cress?" said Reaper before we could leave.

I paused.

"Yes. Do you know something?"

"It's a bit fuzzy," Reaper answered, glancing down, "but now and then I get visions. They're brief and fleeting, but sometimes they give me enough information to be infuriating." He sighed. "It's all part of my punishment, I suppose."

"Right," I said. "Sorry about that. But if you have anything you can give me to go on, I'm all ears."

He nodded and took a deep breath. Then he closed those glowing eyes of his and put his hands on his desk, palms down. Static filled the air. Harvey and I looked at each other. He was about to say something, but I held my index finger up to my mouth to indicate that he should remain silent.

Finally, Reaper gasped and let out a long breath.

"Werewolves," he said raggedly. "She's been taken by werewolves."

That was better than vampires, at least. Unless, of course, the werewolves were planning on having her for dinner. Visions of Rachel à la mode came to mind.

I felt my stomach churn at the thought.

"Any idea where?"

He shook his head.

"Sorry."

"It's okay," I said. "Better than nothing."

"I can tell you that one of the werewolves is…" He trailed off. Then he looked up at me with his glowing eyes. "I don't know exactly. It's just a feeling that he's…different."

"You mean like he digs dudes or something?" I ventured.

If you've never seen a glowy-eyed reaper furrow his or her brow, you've missed out. It was like a unibrow, but with lights.

"I meant that he's unique," Reaper explained after a moment. "Powerful. Angry. Defiant."

"Sounds like every werewolf I've ever met," I stated. "At least when they're in werewolf mode."

Reaper nodded. "That's the thing. I sense that he is perpetually in a state between werewolf form and human form, but…" He stopped again and shook his head. "I don't know. I will say that you'd better be careful or my Order will be fetching you to the other side."

"Swell." It was my turn to sigh. "Okay, well, thanks for the info, Reaper. We'd better be on our way." I then glanced around. "Where's Piper?"

"Down in Processing. I'll tell her you stopped by."

He then got back to work on his papers as I dragged Harvey back to the portal.

"Can you please stick with me and not wander off?" I scolded irritably. "We've got to get to Rachel and I can't be worried about you getting lost."

"Sorry, Chief. I just wanted to thank Reaper again, you know? Plus, we got some good intel from him, right?"

I entered the number again, verified that it said we'd be heading to St. Martin-in-the-Fields, gave Harvey a reluctant nod, and hit the button.

CHAPTER 7

*T*he church was beautiful inside. The dark pews were offset by ivory columns that connected to a domed ceiling. It was covered in gold etchings. Chandeliers hung from chains, taking the eye all the way to the large arched window that sat behind the pulpit.

Some churches went over the top with their ornate designs, but this one just looked elegant.

I wasn't a church-going guy or anything, but I liked the style of this place.

"Let's go," I said, making sure nobody was looking at the null zone area we were in.

We stepped out into the daylight. I'd nearly forgotten about time zones. That would take some getting used to. For all I knew, the PPD here was more on the nightshift like we were in Vegas. That would mean there'd be nothing but a skeleton crew on duty at this time of day. Either way, we had to find them.

"That's a big building," Harvey said as we walked

toward the entrance of the National Gallery. "It's like they crammed a bunch of stuff into as little a spot as they could."

"Well, it's not like England is anywhere near the size of the United States," I noted. "Still, we pack a lot of our museums into D.C. and that's a lot smaller than London."

"Yep."

We headed up the main steps and walked inside.

This place was majorly decked out. There were paintings everywhere, sure, but the architecture was stunning. Details ran along the walls and ceilings. Bas-relief, etchings, inlays, columns...you name it, this place had it. Even the designs on the floors were gorgeous. This place had to have taken forever to build.

A cute blonde in a gray dress approached us.

"Hello," she said in a sweet voice that only served to accentuate her wonderful accent. "Are you from out of town?"

That was one of the oldest pickup lines in the book. If a guy had tried that in this day and age, he would get a response that consisted of a scoff and the rolling of eyes. But I *was* a guy, and she was quite attractive, and her accent caused a tingle in my jibbles, so I was more than happy to let it slide.

But now wasn't the time for pleasantries.

"I am," I replied, "and I'm flattered by the attempt to hook up with me, but I'm currently on a mission."

She squinted at me. "Sorry?"

Harvey nudged my arm and pointed at the badge that was dangling from a holder on her neck.

"She works here, Chief," he whispered.

"Oh." I cleared my throat. "Yes, yes. We are from out of town."

She smiled. "Fantastic. Usually we do tours with larger groups, so if you—"

"Sorry to interrupt," I said while opening my wallet and showing her my PPD badge, "but we're actually in search of your PPD."

She leaned in and studied the badge for a moment. "What's a PPD?"

I hadn't considered the possibility that workers in London might not be as privy to information as the folks in Vegas. Then again, it wasn't like we were in a hotel or anything here.

Just as I was about to answer, another lady stepped over. She was a little older but still quite the looker. Obviously it was good business to pick attractive people to manage tours. A quick study showed a few nicely dressed dudes who had that same swagger going for them as the ladies.

"Patty," said the older woman, "why don't you take my tour over there and I'll work with these gentlemen?"

"As you wish," said Patty at length. "Do you know what a PPD is?"

"It's nothing to be worried about," she replied. "Now, run along. We don't want to keep the tour group waiting, do we?"

"Indeed not," answered Patty. She then gave me a sheepishly naughty grin and a little wave before walking away.

I gave Harvey a look that said, "I *knew* she was hitting on me." His look replied, "Whatever you say, Chief."

"Gentlemen," said the older guide, bringing our attention back to her, "I believe you're in the wrong building."

"We were told to come to the National Gallery in London," I explained.

"And you are looking for the London PPD, correct?"

I glanced at Harvey and then answered, "Yes."

"You are in the wrong building."

That was odd. I never knew Lydia to be incorrect with things. In fact, it had *never* happened. I supposed it could have been due to the fact that we were in a different country here, but that seemed unlikely. We had the internet, after all. Plus, the various PPDs were connected via a wide network of information. Everyone kept everyone in the loop on everything. We had to in the event that the Overworld got overrun by the Netherworld.

"Are you sure?" I asked.

"Young man," she said with a raised eyebrow, "I was in the PPD for many years. I can assure you that I'm quite certain you're in the wrong building."

"According to my AI, it's supposed to be inside the National Gallery."

"It's still in the set, love. It's just not the main galleria."

I gave her another glance, flipping on my amalgamite senses. Sure enough, she was a fae. That explained her good looks.

I gave a quick look at Patty to see if she was also a fae. She wasn't.

"Okay," I acquiesced. "We're in the wrong building. Could you tell us where we're supposed to be?"

"National Gallery Shop."

"Shop?"

"More accurately," she said while leading us back outside, "it's in the back of the Sainsbury Wing where the shop is located." She pointed at the building. "Walk there and turn right. You will pass the large black gates that separate the buildings. There you shall find a null zone, which contains the PPD."

"Thanks," I said.

"And do feel free to contact me again if you happen to need anything else." Her eyes were twinkling. "It's been some time since my last tryst with someone from your side of the pond."

I blinked at her. "I...uh..."

"Have a pleasant day," she replied with a smile before heading back inside.

"You gotta keep your head in the game, Chief," Harvey said as he and I padded down and turned right, seeing the black gates. "I know you're the king of horny and all, but this isn't the time for playing around with the ladies."

My only response was a grimace.

The null zone was at the far end of the building. We stepped through and saw a hidden door there.

"You sure it's okay for us to go in there, Chief?" Harvey asked, looking worried.

"We're PPD officers, Harvey. Any precinct in the world will welcome us with open arms."

"They will?"

I put my hand on the doorknob and hesitated.

"I hope so."

CHAPTER 8

Unlike the Vegas PPD, this place had a number of officers working already. They could have just been paper-pushers, but I couldn't tell by looking at them.

They wore nice suits, which I felt was the way all agents should dress. The mages stood out, wearing their trademarked leather garb, but even they were more dressed like Griff than Rachel. There were no long trench coats in this place, at least none that I could spot.

That made me wonder if Rachel's style of garb had changed.

Interesting.

"May I help you?" asked a young man in a light blue shirt with a dark blue jacket.

"Hi, yes," I said, fumbling a bit. "I'm, uh, Chief Ian Dex from the Las Vegas Paranormal Police Department." I showed him my badge. "Is your chief around?"

"I see," the guy said. "This is about Officer Cress, yes?"

"Right."

"Come this way."

We headed through a building that was double the size of the Vegas PPD but way smaller than the Netherworld one. This place was neatly kept, too, but I still thought our setup was better. Cubicles lined the floor here. Our design allowed for everyone to have their own office. Granted, we had a handful of officers and they had probably a few dozen, but there were always design options, if you cared enough.

"Pardon me, Mr. Bellows," our guide said, "but I have an Officer Ian Dex here from the Las Vegas PPD."

Bellows was a grumpy-looking older man. He had white hair that was parted on the left, hazel eyes, and a ruddy complexion. He wasn't overly large in the middle, but he did look like he could use a few laps around the block. His gray suit jacket was hanging on a coat hook behind his large wooden desk, and his tie of choice was a simple black that lay neatly against his white shirt. His sleeves were also rolled up, which signaled this was a man who had no problem going into the trenches, should the need arise.

My amalgamite senses told me he was a vampire. This was strange, seeing that he looked more gruff than classy.

He gave me an annoyed look and sighed.

"Come in, come in," he said with a wave. "Have a seat."

Harvey and I took the chairs in front of him as he leaned back and crossed his arms, looking askance at me.

"I was told that my former partner, Rachel Cress, was kidnapped."

"Indeed, she was," he replied with a slow blink. "We

have people out looking for her already. We'll let you know when we find something. Now, if you'll be so kind as to—"

I stood up. "I'm here to help find her."

"You have no jurisdiction here, young man."

"I don't care about jurisdiction," I countered hotly. "This is my partner we're talking about."

"Ex-partner," he noted. "And while I applaud your loyalty, I'm afraid you'll just have to allow my finest to do their jobs."

"Yeah, that's not going to work for me."

Bellows stood up and put his hands on his desk. While he was an older guy, I got the feeling that he wasn't someone who was easily subdued. He had scars and everything.

"If you think I'm going to let some pantywaist upstart walk into my office and dictate terms to me, you have seriously misjudged the situation."

"And if you think I'm going to let some geriatric wad of fuckery stop me from finding the most important woman I've ever known, you've seriously got some re-evaluation to do."

We stared eye to eye for a few moments before Harvey stepped up and put his hands on both our shoulders.

"Guys, guys," he said, playing the role of peacemaker, "we're on the same team, remember?"

Bellows and I took our hands off the desk and stood back up, but we didn't break eye contact.

"Now, I know I'm just a rookie and you guys are both chiefs, but I think I have a solution to all of this."

We both looked at Harvey.

"Okay, so Chief Dex here wants to help find his ex-partner, right?"

"Obviously, Harvey," I answered.

"Right. And Chief Bellows, you want to make sure that we're not running around interfering with your day-to-day operations and stuff, yeah?"

"Are you going somewhere with this, young man?"

Harvey swallowed.

"Yeah. Rachel had a partner here, right?"

"She did," Bellows replied. "In a manner of speaking, anyway. The man is a complete arse."

"Was he captured, too?" asked Harvey.

"Unfortunately, no."

"So then he's on his own?"

"He is."

Harvey smiled. "Perfect. Just let us tag around with that guy. He can be in charge and—"

"What?"

"Hear me out, Chief," Harvey said to me. "We'll just be along for the ride. We can give some insights on how Rachel thinks and to provide support where needed."

Bellows licked his lips, showing that he was weighing things.

"No," he said finally with a firm shake of his head. "It's just too much of a risk, especially knowing how you Americans operate."

Just as I was about to open a can of whoop ass on Bellows, Harvey put a hand on my shoulder and gave me a nod.

"Okay, okay," he said, turning back to Bellows. "I have another idea."

Bellows crossed his arms and grimaced. "I haven't all day to bandy about with you two, so make it quick."

"It's simple," my werebear partner stated, "we can either go out on our own and hunt for Rachel, we can work with her partner, or you can deny us the ability to do both and I can pick you up right here in this office, snap you in two, and then stuff you into that garbage pail right there."

Bellows and I both looked taken aback by this, especially because of how calm Harvey had said it.

I nearly laughed.

"My loyalties are to *my* chief, Chief Bellows," Harvey said in a dark voice. "Now, you can kick us out, and you can even put me in jail for ripping you to shreds, but if I go into werebear form right here, you're going to be in a lot of pain for a long, long time." He then put *his* hands on the desk and leaned in menacingly. "Do we have an understanding?"

Bellows swallowed hard and nodded his head.

CHAPTER 9

"So, what did you think?" asked Harvey as we sat in a little waiting room while Bellows had Rachel's partner summoned.

"About what?"

"Good cop, bad cop," he said, as if it were obvious. "I was doing it like those guys from *Starsky & Hutch* used to do."

I assumed this was another show from the seventies, since Harvey had alluded to those over our last couple of months working together.

"Which one were you?" I asked.

"Starsky," he answered.

"No, I mean were you the good cop or the bad cop?"

"The good cop, obviously."

I cocked my head at him. "You threatened to snap the guy in two and shove him into a trash can."

"Well, yeah, but…" He chewed on his lip for a moment.

"Okay, fair enough. Still, though, you have to admit that you were more riled up than I was."

"The guy was trying to block me from helping to save Rachel," I shot back. "Of course I was riled up. Still am, to be honest. If he had come to my precinct saying that his partner had been kidnapped, I would have held out a hand and asked how we could help him."

Harvey merely nodded in response.

"Anyway," I continued, "you did a good job, Harvey. I probably would have gotten there eventually with Bellows, but you easily cut the time in half."

Granted, he'd almost bent Bellows in half, too.

"Thanks, Chief."

He looked uncomfortable. I couldn't tell if it was due to my complimenting him or what, but there was definitely something wrong.

"Something else the matter?"

He looked over at me. "Hmmm?"

"It's like you've suddenly got ants in your pants," I noted, pointing at him. "I'm the one who's supposed to be jittery, not you."

"Oh, it's just a thing with me, is all." He sighed. "I get itchy."

"Ah." I scooted away slightly. "You mean because you're a werebear?"

"Huh?" Then he grimaced. "No, it's not because I'm a werebear. It's because I like dressing the part."

Dressing the part? What was he talking about?

I looked him over. He seemed dressed decently enough from my perspective. No, he wasn't a suit-and-tie guy like me, but his brown dress pants and white shirt fit the bill.

He was staring out into the mass of officers in the station.

Ah, so that was it.

He was feeling underdressed. They all had on suits. He didn't. And since I had on a suit, too, that meant everyone but him was dressed the part.

"Don't worry about it, Harvey," I said gently. "You look fine."

"Chief," he replied while continuing his fidgeting, "we're in London here, not Vegas."

"So?"

"So as a werebear, I already feel out of place."

"I'm sure there are plenty of werebears in London, Harvey."

"That's not what I mean." He stood up and began pacing around. "I've always felt out of place, ever since I was a kid. I'm tall, built big, have a lot of body hair, and I turn into a werebear." He held up a hand at me. "I *know* there are other werebears, but we're kind of rare when compared to werewolves, vampires, fae, pixies, djinn—"

"You don't have to name them all," I declared, "and haven't we had this discussion before?"

"Sort of, but the point is that—aside from weresheep— I'm in the minority here."

"You're talking to the only known amalgamite in existence, Harvey." Then I froze and frowned at him. "Wait, what?"

"What, what?" he said, turning to face me.

"Did you say weresheep?"

"Yeah, why?"

I scanned back through all the courses I'd taken at the academy and there was no mention of weresheep. I shuddered to think how they even managed to come into being, not that werebears or werewolves were any better.

"What the hell are you talking about?"

"You've never heard of weresheep?"

I gave him a stern look. "Apparently not or I wouldn't have said anything."

"True. Well, yeah, there are weresheep."

"Come on. You're kidding me, right?"

"Nope." He leaned back on the wall. "There were even wererabbits at one point, but it was abundantly clear that they were going to overpopulate, so that was nipped in the bud." Harvey then laughed lightly. "If you think *you're* horny, Chief, you should have seen those guys."

"What's their special power?" I queried.

"Wererabbits? Screwing, I'd guess. I mean, seriously, they could go all day."

I rubbed my temples and calmed myself. It was bad enough that I was in London hunting after my ex-partner who had apparently been kidnapped by werewolves, but now I was talking about weresheep with a werebear who was intent on describing the sexual prowess of wererabbits!

"I'm asking about the weresheep, Harvey."

"Oh, right. They kick and bite, but that's about it." He snapped his fingers. "They also grow back their wool really quickly."

"So?"

"So they can run shops for wool and produce it like it's nobody's business."

Insanity. To be fair, I didn't know that zombies were a thing until Shitfaced Fred brought them up to play.

"Anyway, I just don't feel like I fit in, ya know?"

"Again, I'm an amalgamite, Harvey."

"Yeah, but you've learned how to blend." He motioned at my clothing. "You don't stand out like a sore thumb. Hell, when I first met you, Chief, I could have sworn you were a vampire."

I groaned. "Why does everyone think that?"

"Well, look at you," Harvey replied with a chuckle. "You wear the best clothes, your hair is always just right, you keep that five-o-clock shadow running, you're a good-looking dude, and you carry yourself in such a way that tells the world you think your shit doesn't stink."

I wasn't sure whether to feel complimented or offended. On the one hand, everything he said had been true; on the other hand, I didn't want everyone thinking I was a fucking vampire!

But as any good chief would do, I turned my attention back to the problem my subordinate was facing.

"So what do you want to do about it?"

"You looking like a vampire?" he replied. "I don't think it's up to me to do anything about—"

"About *you* feeling uncomfortable, Harvey."

"Oh, right." He shuffled his feet. "Honestly, I'd just like to get an outfit that helps me fit the part."

I nodded at him. That was one thing I could understand.

Power suit.

Harvey would need something properly tailored. If he let me help pick out the perfect outfit, he'd definitely up his street cred. The question was whether or not he'd be able to afford it. I had no problem paying for the outfit, but typically when I made these offers to my officers, they would decline, and I always felt like a pompous ass.

"I can help you out with that," I declared, "but I don't know what your financial situation is, so it may be out of your price range."

"Oh, I'm good on that front, Chief," he replied seriously. "Back before Matilda turned into a real pain in the ass, we had a small business doing decorating for big casinos. I've got enough money in the bank to last a few lifetimes."

I was shocked by this admission.

Harvey did *not* seem the type to have money. Now, I know that *does* make me sound like a pompous ass, but usually you can tell the difference between arrogant wealthy people and people who didn't have much in the bank.

"Seriously?" I said.

"Definitely," he said, smiling. "Don't tell anyone, though, yeah? I wouldn't want people thinking I'm some kind of rich douchebag." He suddenly turned pale. "No offense, Chief."

"I'm not a doucheba—"

The door swung open and a gentleman walked in. He was roughly my height, somewhat slender, had brown hair that was styled just so, a slight tan, and blue eyes that seemed to hold a permanent smirk. He was wearing a black tuxedo with a bowtie. I'd have guessed him to be in his early thirties, but the creases on his forehead marked him as being closer to forty.

"Gentlemen," he said, raising an eyebrow while looking us over. "You're the two Americans, yes?"

"That's right," I said, standing up and offering my hand. "The name's Ian Dex and this is Harvey Smith."

He kept quiet for a moment.

"And you are?" I questioned him.

The guy stood a little taller and said, "Leland. James Leland, 00737."

Harvey was all smiles.

I found this odd, until the werebear spoke.

"You look just like James Bond," he said with a near giddy voice. "It's incredible."

Leland was clearly happy with this response from my partner because his face got even more smug than it was when he'd walked into the room.

"I've always found it best to follow in the footsteps of the greats," Leland stated.

"You *do* realize that James Bond is a fictional character, right?" I said, finding it difficult to *not* want to burst this guy's bubble.

"There's always truth in every fiction, Mr. Dicks."

"Dex."

"Ah, yes. My apologies."

"Dicks is probably more accurate, eh, Chief? I mean, you're always with the ladies and—"

Harvey clearly noted my expression because he clammed up and looked away in horror.

"Anyway," I started, moving the conversation away from James Bond and the fact that my partner thought I should have been named after my prowess in the sack, "you are Rachel's current partner, right?"

His sly face grew even slier. "A gentleman doesn't kiss and tell, Mr. Dex."

"I'm talking about her partner on the PPD, Leland."

"Oh, that. Right. Well, yes, we are…were."

"Were?"

"She's been kidnapped, you know," he said, leaning in.

This guy was obviously a complete boob.

"Yes, I *do* know. That's why we're here."

"Oh, right. Well, we haven't had any solid information on her whereabouts as yet, but there was a note that said she'd been taken."

"Werewolves," I announced. "She was taken by werewolves."

His left eyebrow lowered and his right one went up.

"How do you know this?"

"Let's just say that I have friends in low places," I replied.

"A reaper told us," Harvey said excitedly. "He'd healed my leg after I'd been shot in a parking garage. We were chasing this djinn guy and he possessed me somehow. Anyway, when we—"

"Harvey," I interrupted, barely glancing at my partner, "now is not the time."

"Sorry, Chief."

I took a deep breath.

"Leland, we need to start searching the town for clues regarding werewolf hideouts and such. If you have any ideas on that, we should pursue them. If you have any informants, we should talk to them."

His nod was one of a man who thought his toes were being stepped on. "I know how detective work works, Mr. Dex."

"Then let's get to it," I said with a hint of menace. "My partner is out there in trouble."

"Ex-partner," he amended. Then he sniffed and added, "Honestly, Mr. Dex, I wouldn't have expected such caring from a fellow vampire."

"He's not a fucking vampire," said Harvey sternly. Then he looked at me. "Sorry, Chief. Just trying to be supportive."

My head fell forward.

"Can we just go, please?"

CHAPTER 10

We headed toward the main exit of the London PPD precinct, when Harvey put his hand out and stopped both Leland and me from going any farther.

He pointed.

It was a small shop that contained suits, ties, hats, and other various items that a properly dressed officer should wear. Even I was impressed with the layout. I didn't recall seeing it on the way in, but we hadn't exactly been looking everywhere in the office.

"You have a clothier in your precinct?" I asked with a sense of awe.

"You don't?" Leland replied.

Harvey gave me a gaze that included puppy-dog eyes. He obviously wanted to take care of his clothing situation before we went back out into the field.

"Can I, Chief?" he pleaded.

I wanted to tell him that time was of the essence, but I

doubted another fifteen minutes was going to spell the difference between Rachel's life or death. The werewolves wouldn't do anything to her without first sending a list of demands. Unless, again, they were just planning to eat her. But seeing that there were tons of perfectly tasty people in the world, I assumed her kidnappers had other plans than a simple meal.

"Fine," I replied like a father who was talking to his overzealous teenaged son, "but make it quick."

His face beamed as he ran into the shop.

Honestly, I could have used a new pair of shoes and socks myself. Over the last number of months, I'd run low on them due to all of the damn ubernaturals popping up around Vegas.

That thought was worrisome.

"Lydia," I said through the connector as Leland pressed into the shop and began looking at ties, "is everything okay there?"

"It's fine, sweetie," she replied. "I've been keeping my ears open for anything new on the Strip, but nothing has happened yet. The crew isn't due in for another few hours."

"Good, good." I licked my lips. "I'm sure they can handle anything that comes their way."

"Of course they can, honey." Her voice was gentle. Obviously she knew the stress I was under. "How are things there?"

"Interesting," I replied quickly. "Harvey's being a mixture of helpful and annoying."

"So, helpfully annoying, or annoyingly helpful?"

"Exactly," I answered. "And Rachel's partner is a real piece of work. He thinks he's James Bond."

"That sounds lovely," she said.

Sometimes her algorithms didn't quite pick up on my sarcasm.

"Well, if anything comes up, don't hesitate to contact me, okay?"

"Of course, sugar," she said. "And if you need anything from the crew here, they're only a couple of portal jumps away."

"Speaking of that," I said, snapping my fingers, "you should know that the London PPD is not exactly in the National Gallery building."

"I know, puddin'," she stated smoothly. "They're located at the back of the building next door, but it *is* still part of the Gallery."

"Right." Even my AI had to be difficult at times. "Okay, well, I've got to get back to it, Lydia."

"Be careful, lover."

"Sure thing."

I disconnected and set about studying the *Wanted* posters on the wall. It didn't seem much different than what we had at the Vegas PPD, aside from the fact that there were far more faces. Granted, London was a larger city than Vegas, but there were easily ten times as many posters here. That explained why this precinct was crammed with officers, and it also explained why Bellows was wound so tight.

That made me feel kind of bad for how we'd treated the poor guy.

Still, with all this mess, you'd have thought he'd *want* the help.

By the time I'd gotten to the third row of faces, Leland and Harvey stepped out of the shop.

"You've got to be kidding me," I said at the vision of my partner.

"You like it?" he asked hopefully.

Imagine a nearly seven-foot tall, hairy, burly guy wearing a brown tweed deerstalker cap, a matching trench coat with the collar up, a pipe in one hand, and a large magnifying glass in the other.

"Sherlock Holmes, I presume?" I said in a really bad British accent.

Harvey was all smiles.

"So you *do* like it?"

I wanted to tell him that he looked like a fool, but I just didn't have the heart. It was clear he was greatly enjoying his look. And, to be fair, seeing as how he was standing next to a man who thought he was James Bond...well, it just worked. Frankly, they probably should have been partners.

"It's great, Harvey," I said with a shake of my head. "You're really something, you know that?"

"Thanks, Chief." He was very excited. "I was going to go with the top hat instead of the deerstalker, but I'm already pretty tall and so I figured it'd be knocked off my head wherever we walked. Besides, this feels more authentic to the original character."

"Oh, most definitely," I agreed, trying not to lay the sarcasm on too thick. "All you need now is a Dr. Watson and you'll be all set."

He took the pipe out of his mouth. "You want to play that part, Chief?"

"Um, no. I only play dress-up with the ladies, Harvey." I went to turn away but stopped myself. "And don't go getting any ideas about trying to find someone to *actually* be your Dr. Watson. We don't have time for that. Understood?"

"I got it, Chief," he replied, looking a little disappointed.

This was definitely going to be an odd adventure, and we'd certainly stick out like a sore thumb, but that may not be such a bad thing. It was better for our prey to focus on these two, thinking they were part of some weird acting entourage, than it was for them to be on the lookout for actual PPD officers.

With one last glance over my two partners in law, I said, "It's time to get moving."

CHAPTER 11

S ure enough, everyone was staring at Leland and
Harvey as we walked through Trafalgar Square.
It didn't bother me in the least since the attention was
focused solely on them and not me. They, on the other
hand, seemed to relish the attention.

"Where are we going?" I asked Leland.

"Down Whitehall," he replied, pointing. "There is a
McDonald's that way."

"That'd be great," said Harvey. "I'm starving."

Leland nodded at him. "Which is all well and good, but
the purpose of our visit is to speak with one of my
contacts."

"And you haven't already done this?"

"Of course I have," he answered tightly. "However, she
is the type of lady who only provides information for
special favors, and last I spoke with her, I was already
spent from a previous fling."

"Favors?"

"Yes, Mr. Dex." His grin was of the naughty nature. "Most of my contacts are of the female persuasion. I give them a little something of what they need and they reply in kind with a bit of information."

"I see," I said, appraising Leland in an entirely new light.

Actually, I kind of liked this idea. Back in Vegas, my informants either wanted cash or expected me to help them out of parking tickets and such. If I could line up a bunch of chicks that I could bone in exchange for intel, that'd be a win-win, for sure.

"I like this idea of yours, Leland," I said finally. "I'll have to start using that back home, too."

His face changed to one of concern and he slowed his pace until we stopped.

"Listen, old boy," he said in a mentoring way, "it's not my place to tell a fellow officer how to run his jurisdiction, but it takes a special touch to manage things the way I do here."

"What do you mean?"

He wiped some lint from his right sleeve. "Ladies expect a certain level of seduction that few men are able to provide."

"Oh boy," said Harvey, clearly recognizing that Leland didn't know exactly who I was.

"Ah," I said, giving Harvey a wink. "Well, I'll just have to watch and see what you do. Nothing better than learning from the master, right?"

Leland adjusted his bowtie proudly at the comment. He then gave me another onceover and nodded. I wanted to slap that raised eyebrow right off his face, but for now I'd let him do his thing.

We needed information.

I didn't care how we got it.

"I guess my first lesson," I added, unable to control myself as we moved back down the road, "is to shack up with ladies who frequent McDonald's."

"You have to have contacts in many walks of life, Mr. Dex," Leland said in stride, either not realizing I was chiding him or not caring. "It's uncommon to find informants on the wealthy side of town, I'm afraid."

He had me there. Most of the upperclass were the ones in on nefarious ventures. They didn't often inform on each other, either, especially since they all had far too much dirt to spread around.

"Fair enough."

We arrived at McDonald's and found a number of customers walking in and out.

"Want anything, Chief?"

"No, thank you," I answered as we all stepped inside. "I'm careful as to what I put into my body."

"That's not what Serena said," Harvey stated. Then he blinked a few times. "Oh, you mean food?"

It was becoming more and more trying to deal with my new partner.

"Just go eat, will you? And be quick about it."

He nodded and got in line.

I turned to spot Leland speaking with a middle-aged woman who was not exactly what you'd call a looker. She had straggly hair, tired eyes, and was rather plump. Still, there was a certain cuteness about her that I found somewhat appealing, but I had a tendency to find something intoxicating in every woman I met. Ladies just did it for me. Big, small, plain, extravagant…there was always a bit of oomph in every type.

I moved over to Leland, but he gave me a look that said, "Stay back, I'm working."

So I took the table next to them and listened in.

"I know I wasn't feeling randy the other day, love," he said, "but you must understand that mine is a trying business."

"That's what you said then, yeah? Didn't help my situation though, now did it?"

He cleared his throat.

"My dear, you must imagine how wonderful things will be now that I have an hour of free time and am feeling rested and ready."

An hour? I didn't want to wait another hour.

"Excuse me," I said, tapping her on the shoulder, "but do you know anything about the disappearance of an Officer Rachel Cress?"

"What are you doing, Mr. Dex?" Leland said with dark eyes. "This is *my* informant."

"An hour is too long, Leland," I replied. "If she knows information, I can get it out of her in thirty seconds."

She scoffed at my proclamation. "I don't know who you are, mister, but I'm not just going to give up information I know without a bit of—"

I reached out again and touched her arm, allowing a flow of amalgamite energy to enter her body.

Her eyes grew wide for a moment as her mouth formed the words, "Oh, my God." Within seconds, she was shuddering and making cooing sounds. Fifteen seconds in, the entirety of McDonald's was staring at her as she melted in the throes of passion.

With a final, "Ahhhh!," I let go of her arm and gave Leland a look so full of smugness that he sat back in shock.

"That guy," the woman said through ragged breaths as she pointed at a young man who was seated near the exit.

He was staring in our direction.

Of course, so was everyone else.

But I pinned him instantly as being a werewolf.

"He knows where she is," the woman said again, sounding both exhausted and thoroughly satisfied.

I stood up, but she grabbed my arm.

"Come back anytime, lover," she said. "I'll tell you anything you want to know."

"Me, too," said an old lady who was sitting at the next table.

I gently pushed her arm away from me while smiling at the two women.

When I looked back up, I saw that our werewolf pal was exiting the joint at full burn.

"Harvey," I called out, "we've got a runner."

"But my food, Chief."

"Let's go!"

"Damn it!"

CHAPTER 12

We bolted toward the door, but there were a couple of older folks coming in who were in our way.

I smiled anxiously at them until they finally got past the entrance.

The old man said, "Many thanks, young fellow. It's not often that people take the time to help the elderly these days, you know?"

"It's no problem, sir," I said, desperately wanting to get out of the building.

"When I was a youth, we were taught proper manners." He leaned in with a serious look. "You respected your elders back then or you got your hide tanned."

"I would imagine so, yes."

He shook his head while looking off into the distance. "Ah, but the youth of today are nothing but a bunch of dodgy twits."

"Yes," I said, feeling certain that I'd lost my chance to catch up to the werewolf at this point. "I'm sure they are. Listen, I'm sorry, but I really need to—"

"Most of them should be at Her Majesty's Pleasure, if you catch my meaning."

"Not really, no."

That's when I sensed something was off. The old woman hadn't moved and she appeared to be blocking the exit on the other side.

I gave both of them a deeper look.

Werewolves.

"Damn it," I said, pushing past the old bullshitters and out onto the sidewalk, turning on the jets in the process.

Unfortunately, I slammed into a person walking in the other direction.

We both hit the ground.

"Hey," the guy said while dusting off his suit, "watch where you're going, will you? This suit is worth more than..." He paused and looked at me just as I was looking at him. "Ian Dex?" he said, rubbing his eyes as he got to his feet.

"Simon Strong?" I looked up and saw another man standing there. "Montague?"

"Officer Dex," Montague replied with a short nod. "Always a pleasure."

"Thanks," I said while pushing myself back up. "What are you guys doing here?"

Simon waved a dismissive hand. "Mages summoning demons, making a power play to destabilize the balance. You?"

"Rachel got herself kidnapped by werewolves."

"Shit," said Simon. "Wish we could help, but you know how it is with mages and demons."

"Never ends, does it?"

"No."

"Pardon me," said Montague, "but there was a fellow who sped by us about thirty seconds ago." He glanced back. "I still see him running towards the square. Is he the one you're after?"

"Actually, yeah," I said.

Montague gestured and formed a silvery orb. With a word, he released it. It raced through the crowded street until it crashed into the back of the fleeing man, causing him to spasm and fall to the ground.

"He'll be down for a few minutes," Montague said with a nod.

"Thanks, man," I said. "You're a lifesaver."

"Say, Dex," Simon said, "I don't mean to pry, but you have James Bond and an industrial version of Sherlock Holmes standing behind you."

I gave him a look that said "help me" and then said, "I know."

Simon stepped around me and nodded. "Great seeing you, Ian." He then glanced at his watch. "Well, we have a lot of destruction to do and not a lot of time to do it. Good seeing you again."

"Good seeing you again," I said in agreement. "Thanks again for the help, Montague."

"Think nothing of it."

We took off to catch our werewolf pal before he woke up from whatever it was that Montague had cast on him. It certainly made me think that I'd have been wiser to bring along one of the mages rather than a werebear. Another glance at Harvey in his silly outfit solidified that thought even further.

I dragged the runner to his feet as he mumbled something incoherent. Obviously Montague's spell had knocked the shit out of him.

We moved to the wall and I told Harvey and Leland to keep watch.

"This is *my* case, Mr. Dex," Leland said sternly. "It should be me who is questioning this fellow."

"You can do that when I'm done," I replied before smacking the werewolf. "Unless you want to end up in an early grave, pal," I said to the dazed guy, "you'd better tell me what you know about the disappearance of Rachel Cress."

"Ouch," he answered, rubbing his cheek. "No reason to hit me."

"Americans," Leland grunted. "So uncivilized."

"Excuse me?"

"May I?" Leland said, motioning toward the werewolf.

I didn't know why, but I backed away.

"Listen, old chap," said Leland as he helped straighten up the man's outfit, "we Brits need to stick together. Do you agree?"

He continued rubbing his jaw. "I guess so."

"We've a duty to Queen and Country, I'd say," Leland continued. "Our national pride is at stake on a daily basis. If we don't keep our guard up, we'll be at the mercy of countries like my new friend's here in no time."

"That makes sense," the werewolf said, looking unsure. "Where are you going with all of this?"

"It's simple, really. You provide me the details on the whereabouts of Officer Cress and I'll be sure to put in a good word for you, my fellow countryman, so that they are lenient on your sentencing."

The guy gave Leland a hard stare, then glanced at me, then up at Harvey, and finally back at Leland.

"And who's going to stop the Werewolves of London Clan from tearing me to shreds when I get out of prison?" His look was laced with expectancy. "Assuming they don't just have me done in while I'm jailed, that is."

"I'm sure we can work something out," Leland said after a moment of hesitation.

So much for his patriotism play.

"Yeah, I don't think so," the werewolf said.

"Hmmm." Leland pursed his lips. "Do it for the Queen?"

"No."

I pulled out Boomy and stuck it on the guy's forehead.

With a dark look, I growled, "Do it to avoid having parts of your head littering the street?"

"Okay, okay," he said, swallowing hard as his eyes crossed in an effort to study the Desert Eagle that was threatening to ruin his day. "I'll take you to her."

I left Boomy pressed against his head for another few moments and then pushed it a little harder before letting go.

"If there are any tricks," I stated in a tight voice, "I'll shoot you more than once."

CHAPTER 13

*W*e took a brisk walk down Northumberland Avenue. I didn't know where our new pal was taking us, mostly because I wasn't familiar with the area, but Boomy was at the ready, just in case it was some kind of nefarious play on his part.

Buses and cars were zipping by this way and that as the bustle of people who were going about their everyday lives seemed bent on impeding our progress.

Again, I had to remind myself that Rachel would be fine until the demands came in. Hopefully, anyway. My gut churned at the thought that she may be tortured, though.

That only hardened my resolve.

"Keep moving," I said, sticking Boomy into the guy's back.

He grunted in reply but picked up his pace.

"It's that way," he said as we neared an intersection.

"The alley right between The Sherlock Holmes and Thai Square Spa."

"Hey, Chief," Harvey said with excitement while pointing at The Sherlock Holmes restaurant, "you think we could—"

"No," I interrupted before he could finish.

"Aw, come on, Chief."

I stopped and turned on my partner.

"Look, Harvey, this isn't some vacation that we're on here. My partner—"

"Ex-partner," Leland corrected.

"—has been kidnapped by werewolves. If she gets hurt in any way, that would be pretty awful, don't you think?"

"Of course, Chief."

"And every moment that we're wasting, stopping to play dress-up and looking for ways to stuff our faces with fast-food, is another moment that Rachel could be suffering through some kind of torture." I stopped while staring at the large man. "Do you really want that on your conscience?"

The werewolf began edging away from us, but I spotted him doing so out of the corner of my eye.

I raised Boomy in his direction while keeping my gaze on Harvey.

Mr. Werewolf froze in place.

"All right, Chief," Harvey said like a kid who'd just been routed for getting a failing grade in math. "You're right. I've been acting like a fool."

He moved to take off his hat, but Leland stopped him.

"Nonsense," the James Bond wannabe stated. "You are following in the tradition of a fellow who has solved more intricate cases than any sleuth in the history of crime. Who are we if not those we wish to be?"

My eyebrows uncontrollably squeezed together.

"What?"

"You, Mr. Dex, are obviously a stickler for rules, and that—"

"I'm really not," I stated, interrupting him this time.

"Well, you sure are on this day."

"My partner—*your* partner—is in trouble, Leland." I smacked myself on the side of my head as I lowered Boomy. "Doesn't that bother you in the least?"

He looked quite offended at my remark.

"Of course it does," he said. "What gentleman would feel less than concerned over the current disposition of a delicate flower such as Rachel Cress?"

I blinked and shook my head as if someone had just thrown a bucket of freezing water on me.

"Are we talking about the same Rachel Cress?"

Leland rolled his eyes. "I speak of the female form in generalities, Mr. Dex. Police work is a man's world."

"Wow," I nearly choked in reply. "That's probably not something you want the 'delicate' Rachel Cress to ever hear you say. She'll end up kicking you right in your double-oh-sevens."

He cleared his throat and scanned the area as if she may have been close enough to have heard him. His hands even moved to protect himself. Obviously, he had been through this before.

"Yes, I'm aware of her feelings on the matter."

"Uh, Chief?"

"What, Harvey?"

"The guy's gone."

I spun to where our werewolf pal had been standing a moment before. Sure enough, he'd split.

"Fucking fuck, fuck," I spat.

While I didn't want to point fingers at either Harvey or Leland, it *was* their goddamned fault that the guy got away. Technically, I suppose it was my fault for letting them take my focus off the matter at hand.

I glared at them both.

"All right, you two," I said through gritted teeth, "this stops here. You're going to quit with this charade and help me find Rachel or you're going to get the hell out of my hair. One way or the other."

Harvey went to take off his hat again.

"I don't care about the outfit, Harvey. What I *do* care about is the lack of professionalism. Interfere with my progress once more and I swear I'll send your ass straight back to Vegas." I met his eyes. "Got it?"

He gulped. "Got it."

"As for you, Leland, I can't dictate what you do or do not do, but if you impede my progress toward finding Rachel again, you can expect a really nice shoe to be buried in your *arse*." I said that last word in his manner of speaking, to drive the point home. "Are we clear?"

He merely harrumphed, never taking his eyes away from mine.

I had to give him his due there. It wasn't often that a person would dare stand toe to toe with me on such a threat. I could look very menacing when I wanted to, after all.

"There he is, Chief," Harvey said, pointing to the alley by The Sherlock Holmes restaurant.

We ran out into the street, dodging cars as their drivers laid on their horns.

I made sure to grab Harvey's arm as we sped by the restaurant that was the namesake of his current getup. Patrons in the windows were pointing and laughing at him as we padded on by. It was probably the highlight of their day, especially if there were any tourists in there.

We got through the little alley and chased our werewolf pal on Craven until he jumped down a set of stairs by one of the buildings.

It was a null zone.

"Trap," I said, holding back Bond and Holmes before they could jump in after our prey. "Get your weapons out."

Harvey pulled out his Desert Eagle. Leland unveiled a Walther PPK.

While officers didn't go about flaunting the fact that they carried weapons, the PPD didn't follow any standard societal rules. We did our best to keep things under wraps, of course, but our job required the use of guns and other weaponry in order to subdue supernatural perps.

"Nice gun," I said with a genuine nod at Leland. It wasn't a commonly used weapon in the PPD, but it had a certain level of class to it. "I'm impressed."

"Authenticity, Mr. Dex."

"Right." I checked Boomy to make sure he was fully loaded.

Then he looked at Boomy with wide eyes. "Is your gun big enough?"

I wanted to make a juvenile wisecrack in response, but it was too easy.

"Best gun I've ever owned," I replied proudly. Then I pointed at his PPK. "I'm assuming you're using standard breaker bullets?"

"No," he answered. "We received a new line of breakers that are multi-infused. Some pixie in America put the plans up and everything has been altered accordingly."

"That pixie works for me," I stated proudly. "Now, am I to assume you know how to use your PPK as well as your famous James Bond?"

"Let's just say that I rarely miss."

"Good enough for me."

We jumped into the null zone.

CHAPTER 14

The area was dark and damp, but it was also a lot more roomy than I'd expected.

I reached out to feel the area and wasn't all that happy with what I was sensing.

Werewolves.

If my radar was right, there were about fifteen of them, including the guy who'd led us down here.

He'd be the first to die.

"Welcome, Mr. Dex," said Mr. Werewolf as he stepped out into the light. I held my trigger finger back. "I have to say that I didn't expect you'd actually follow me into a null zone, but I was hoping you would."

"Where's Rachel?" was all I cared to say in response.

"Not here," he answered with a teasing grin. "But she won't matter to you anyway, unless you get past us, of course."

I frowned at him. "Call me dumb—"

"Okay," he said quickly.

"—but is this some kind of game to you?"

"Most certainly," Werewolf-boy said, nodding. "We call it the challenge game. It helps us to know who is truly at the top of the heap. And you're the perfect candidate for helping us with this because we all know what you are, Mr. Dex."

"And what's that, exactly?"

He tilted his head. "An amalgamite, of course. We also know that you're one of a kind. This means that we, as werewolves, wish to test our mettle against you." He then looked over Harvey and Leland. "Your friends can play, too, of course, but they're not really going to be much trouble. We'll dispose of them quickly." He then studied Harvey again. "He may be a bit of a struggle, I'll admit, but your James Bond lookalike should have informed his next of kin before entering the area."

I ignored that. "And what if I refuse to participate in your challenge game?"

"Then you'll die and so will Officer Cress."

Right, so I had to allow a bunch of werewolves to test themselves against me in order to get to Rachel. I didn't know if they had any expectations about me dropping Boomy and doing this in a hand-to-hand fashion, but that wasn't going to happen.

"And so we start with killing everyone in here?" I said, letting my senses flow. "Is that right?"

"If you can, Mr. Dex," he replied smugly. "If you c—"

That's all he got out before Boomy ended his thought process.

An instant later, there were wolves jumping at us from all angles.

I'd taken down three of them almost as fast as they appeared, but the rest were coming in quicker than I could manage. At this rate, Boomy would become nothing more than a club.

Harvey had morphed partially into werebear mode, which looked truly ridiculous since his Holmes outfit was still on his person. My guess was that his precious new outfit wasn't magically protected from shredding. He must have either known this or was worried about it because he should have completed the switchover by now.

I rolled back as a werewolf launched at me, aiming for where I'd been a moment before. A round from Boomy squelched his menacing thoughts, but another wolf was already on my leg, working to tear into my flesh. Fortunately, I was not that easy to rip apart. It still hurt like hell to be bitten, sure, but it wasn't like the doggy was going to do too much damage. This became even more true as I pressed Boomy against its head, yelled, "Quit biting me, you fucker," and pulled the trigger.

Harvey roared and threw two wolves with such force that they thudded against a wall and slid down with lifeless eyes. Trails of blood smeared the concrete behind them.

Leland was also holding his own, and he was true to his word.

The man could shoot.

I'd always prided myself on being quite the marksman, but this guy was in a class all by himself. He was firing that PPK as if it were an extension of his person. Honestly, it was mesmerizing to watch, which was a problem because another werewolf slammed into my side and did its best to bite my head off.

If you've ever smelled the breath of an aging Chihuahua, take that and multiply it by ten. Then, get that stench all slobbered into your hair and your five-thousand-dollar suit. Finally, let those stinky teeth fight to prick your skin.

Now, how do you think that would make you feel?

It pissed me off.

"Son of a bitch," I yelled as I pried the nasty jaws from my head. "Gingivitis much?" I said while angrily shoving Boomy into the beast's mouth and pulling the trigger.

That wasn't the best idea I'd ever had, seeing that I was covered in its nastiness within seconds.

"Ah!"

I looked back to see that Leland was grappling with one of the wolves, and he wasn't very good at it, either. In fact, I would go as far as to say that Leland didn't know how to fight at all. Mostly, he just lay on his back, slamming his fists against the creature's head as if he were playing the bongos. It was so bad that the werewolf started laughing.

Harvey, on the other hand, had dropped a few more of the doggies, leaving only two left...aside from the one that Leland was basically petting.

"Harvey," I yelled, pointing at Leland.

My partner leaped across the expanse and grabbed the wolf off the James Bond clone. Then he snapped its neck with a solid roar.

I tagged one of the two remaining wolves in the side of the head with perfectly placed shots from Boomy.

The final wolf had taken off into the shadows, but while I was definitely interested in chasing him and ending his ability to consume oxygen, I couldn't help but feel we'd just be running into another trap.

No, it was time to regroup, especially since I now had a little more information to go on.

"Aren't we going to chase him, Chief?" Harvey asked, his voice a little deeper than usual. "He'll get away."

"No need," I said as I tucked Boomy back into his holster. "We know what they want now and that means they're not going to hurt Rachel until they get it."

"You?" asked Leland with a nod as he worked to remove the saliva from his hair. His hands were cut up pretty bad. "They want you."

"Yep," I sighed as I also did my best to scrape the goop from my person.

Honestly, I should either choose a different line of work or I should start dressing like Warren. At least then I wouldn't give a damn about getting covered in all this crap.

CHAPTER 15

*W*e walked back out of the null zone and up the stairs that took us back to Craven Street.

I had enough information to go on at this point to make me believe that Rachel wasn't going to be killed unless I was killed. While I had no intention of dying, I felt better knowing that these wolves all wanted to challenge me. Okay, maybe "felt better" isn't the right way to to put it. The point was that I understood their perspective. They were always looking to see who was the top-dog in the bunch. If one of them bested me, he or she would be the alpha for some time to come. The dogs were smart about it, too. They knew I'd come to Rachel's aid, which meant they were all in on this challenge game of theirs. It gave me little choice but to participate.

That made me raise an eyebrow at myself. Sometimes my self-talk was less than helpful.

Sniff.

The word came into my mind out of nowhere. It was another one of Gabe the Vampire's little treats, just like *Time* and *Flashes* had been. Also like those, there was no user manual with this one.

Sniff, it came again.

"What do we do now, Chief?" asked Harvey.

We were just standing at the top of the stairs, staring down toward where The Sherlock Holmes restaurant sat.

"I say we go back to the PPD and gather our wits about us," suggested Leland as he dabbed a handkerchief against his bloodied lip.

Harvey seemed to agree. "You guys got a vending machine there?"

"Quite a lovely one, in fact," answered Leland.

I tuned the two of them out as I studied the area. There were flowers and bushes in little pots sitting on small wrought iron balconies along the two rows of flats on either side. To our right, anyway. A more industrial feel ran to our left.

Sniff.

Yes, I was fighting to ignore the command. However, I was starting to get the point that, on some cosmic level, these special abilities spoke to me. It was like they were telling me the best time to use them. How they knew that, I couldn't say, but seeing that they'd been right every time, except for when I'd slowed the world to watch Dr. Vernon have an orgasm—and it should be noted that *I* thought it was exactly the right time to use that particular skill—I thought it may be wise to listen.

So as the two goobers continued blathering on about

vending machines and their favorite detectives from the past, I rolled my eyes and sniffed.

Nothing happened.

Then I remembered that I had to *think* the word actively for it to work.

I sighed.

Sniff, I thought in that magical way that seemed to activate any of the skills Gabe provided.

The world suddenly became a haven of smells. Flowers, car fumes, colognes, perfumes, food, birds, buildings, the street, and Harvey. These were the things that stood out most. Especially Harvey. Werebears weren't exactly known for smelling like roses.

Obviously I would need to focus this *Sniff* skill or I'd end up gagging.

I was looking for Rachel, so I needed to recall her scent.

As if I were seeing an aromatic photograph of my ex-partner, my nose picked up something. It was as clear as day, making me feel compelled to start running toward the source.

"Where're you going, Chief?" Harvey called out, but I was too far gone to pay much attention to him. "Wait up!"

I chased the scent all the way down to the Strand, anxiously waited for a break in the traffic, and then bolted for Duncannon. If I had been an actual dog at this point, I'd be roadkill. I now understood why dogs didn't pay much attention to anything else once they were on a scent trail. It was overwhelming.

To our right was St. Martin-in-the-Fields again. It was as if we'd come full circle.

But the scent wasn't in the church. It was beside it somewhere.

I kept running, doing all I could not to throw people out of my way in the process. While my nose was going insane with the need to find the source of the smell, my forebrain had to keep my wits about it. If I didn't, I'd probably cause a lot of injuries.

"Chief," Harvey said raggedly, "what's going on?"

I pushed his hand from my shoulder as we approached a statue.

This was where the trail ended. The Edith Cavell monument.

Like a man possessed, I jumped up and started climbing the front of it. It was tough to get a foothold, but I managed, scaring away a number of pigeons in the process.

"Chief?"

I looked down at him and snarled.

"Okay, okay," he said, holding up his hands in surrender. "No need to bite my head off."

Obviously having a nose like this made for a powerful animal response. But I didn't feel bad about it. He could clearly see I was on to something, so why pester the shit out of me?

I pulled myself up until I was face to face with the namesake of the monument.

Sitting atop her head was a brown leather glove.

It was Rachel's.

In fact, it was one of the gloves that I'd given to her on our first anniversary working together before I was the chief.

I dropped down and held it up to Harvey in an effort to explain why I'd been so focused on my running.

He squinted at it for a second and then took out his magnifying glass to give it a deeper study.

"Looks like a glove," he said finally.

"Yes," agreed Leland, "I would most definitely say that's a glove."

I just stood there staring back and forth between them.

"Obviously it's a glove, you idiots," I said with more heat than was necessary. "The point is that it's *Rachel's* glove."

"Really?" Harvey pulled up his magnifying glass again.

"Honestly, Harvey," I said while pulling the glove away, "how do you expect that your magnifying glass is going to help you determine the validity of my statement?"

He lowered the glass with a sad look.

"Sorry, Chief."

Rookie or not, there *was* something known as common sense.

"I thought the use of the glass was a wise one," Leland said, patting my partner on the shoulder. "There's never enough detailed study one can do when seeking out answers, you know."

I scoffed. "You two should partner up."

"At least he wouldn't yell at me as much," Harvey more mumbled than said.

He was right, though. I was being kind of hard on him.

Wait—no, I wasn't!

I was all about having fun, sharing laughs, and being zany, but there's a time and place for actual work, too. Now, I knew that Harvey *thought* he was working while studying Rachel's glove with his Sherlock Holmes fan kit, but the fact was that it wouldn't help. He should know that. This wasn't some cosplay convention we were at. This was real.

Still…

"I just need you to think, Harvey," I said in as calm a voice as I could manage at the moment. "May I see the glass, please?"

He tentatively handed it over.

"Now, I ask you if using this ancient piece of sleuthing technology would really help when studying this glove?" I held up the glove and looked through the glass at it as if to prove a point. That's when I noticed a tiny stream of text that read, 'The Chandos' on it. "I'll be damned."

"What is it, Chief?" asked Harvey.

"What is The Chandos?" I said to Leland, ignoring Harvey's question.

"It's a pub," our James Bond clone replied while pointing behind me.

I spun around and noted that the place was right on the corner. It had a wooden outside with columns framing the entryway, and it read "29 St. Martin's Lane" in the center.

"Huh," I said, casually handing the magnifying glass back to Harvey.

"So it came in useful, eh, Chief?" he said accusingly.

My shoulders dropped. "I suppose it did."

"Uh huh."

CHAPTER 16

*I*t was your standard pub with lots of deep, dark wood that was shined and polished. There were mirrors lining the wall behind a fully stocked bar, and a number of seating areas where people could spend their nights drinking away their sorrows. Right now, though, all the patrons seemed to be having a pleasant time.

"It says they have a menu..." started Harvey, but he stopped when I gave him a dull look. "Sorry, Chief. Just hungry."

"They've got nice fish and chips," Leland noted.

I looked over them both. Seriously, they belonged together. I couldn't even imagine how Rachel had managed to put up with Leland over these last couple of months. She probably arranged to have herself kidnapped in order to get away from the guy.

"Fine," I said, throwing up my hands, "you two have a

seat and get some food. I'm going to keep using this nose of mine to find more information."

"You sure, Chief?"

"Oh, I'm sure." I then cleared my throat at the realization that I'd said that quite pompously. "If anything happens, I'll use the connector to reach you."

Harvey was all smiles now.

"We'll be here if you need us." Then his smile turned to a serious look. "Do you want to bring my magnifying glass? Just in case?"

I didn't, but damn if it hadn't been useful back at the statue. It took everything I had not to roll my eyes as I swiped the glass from his hand and slipped it into my suit pocket.

"I'll be back shortly."

Without waiting, I moved smoothly through the tables and people until I spotted a null zone. Actually, it was a guess because everyone was giving it a wide berth as they walked by it. A deeper look showed that I was correct.

Behind it was a blank wall. There had to be something to it, though, because one didn't just go around putting null zones in a building without there being some purpose to it. I grumbled and took out the magnifying glass and started going over every inch of the thing until I spotted two sets of contact points. One on each side. It was a door. My guess was that there was no knob because we were in a pub. Translation: If a drunkard happened by, they may not be as impacted by a null zone, and so they might just twist the knob and walk on in.

I tucked the glass away.

Another win for Mr. Holmes, and Harvey.

The door opened after I pressed the contacts at the same time.

Also at that moment, I felt the *Sniff* sense dissipate. But I no longer needed it to know I was on the right track. This was apparent because of the item sitting on a small table in the middle of the moderately-sized room I'd entered.

It was Rachel's badge.

I picked it up and looked it over.

Instead of the "Las Vegas Paranormal Police Department," this one just read "P.P.D." along the top and a redundant "Paranormal Police Department" around the rest of it. All of the PPD stations had been going to the generalized form instead of employing the locale. My precinct hadn't been forced down that path yet because we were too small and we rarely got new recruits. In fact, Harvey was the first since the last rookie had joined the Vegas PPD...which had been me.

"Welcome to your doom, Mr. Dex," said the powerful voice of a woman who had stepped out of the shadows. It was an American accent, too. "Your capabilities are quite impressive, I must say."

She was built like someone who spent a fair amount of time in the gym, compact and muscular with a hint of femininity that threatened to turn my frown upside down. Though she was a little shorter than I considered practical for playing a domineering role, her demeanor radiated strength and confidence.

In a nutshell, she was my kind of woman.

"When you welcome me to my doom," I said, slowly

placing Rachel's badge back on the table, "do you mean that in a nefarious way or a naughty one?"

"Is there a difference?"

"Only in that naughty ends in our mutual pleasure while nefarious ends in only one of us feeling sated."

She licked her lips as her teeth started to grow and her face began to elongate.

"Nefarious it is," I said.

I backed toward the door while reaching out to see if she was alone.

Surprisingly, she was.

There were only moments left between her going full wolf and me having a shot at making a move.

So I changed tactics and lunged at her.

She tried to dive away, but being in the middle of her morphing phase made her as vulnerable as I got when trying to employ skills like *Haste*. Her changeover would be quicker than mine, in comparison, but it wasn't quick enough.

I grabbed her shoulders and dumped a ton of amalgamite sexual energy into her, easily double the amount I'd filled the chick with back at McDonald's.

She howled and stopped transitioning. It wouldn't reverse her, but interrupting the process at all would at least keep her vulnerable.

Her eyes were wide with passion and her breathing was shallow and quick. If it weren't for the fact that she currently looked like the love child of a pygmy and a giant wolf, I'd be really digging this at the moment.

She howled again, reminding me to let her go.

I was dumping *way* too much energy into her, which

brought an entirely new meaning to the term "doggie style."

Ew.

I backed away and she looked at me hungrily. Not in the way that werewolves usually looked at people either. I mean that *other* way.

"I underestimated you," she said, drooling. It wasn't attractive. "I had expected we would fight hand to hand, but you have ignited a fire in me that usually only happens when I'm in heat."

Again, ew.

I pulled out Boomy and pointed it at her.

"Ah," she growled seductively, "I guess it's *you* who gets to play nefariously?"

"Considering that you've already had your happy ending," I replied with a bit of swagger, "I'd argue naughty is more apropos, especially since I have no intention of killing you."

She raised an eyebrow at my proclamation.

"Oh?"

"I will, if I have to, but I'm hoping you'll be cooperative instead."

Her response was a rumbling laugh and a shaking of her head. She then scratched her ear very fast. Fortunately, she used her hand for this. If she had used her foot, I'd have thought that far too silly.

"You have already conquered me, Mr. Dex," she admitted without shame. "I am yours to do with as you please."

"Yeah, okay," I said, realizing that I'd cheated in order to "conquer" her.

The saying that "all is fair in love and war" is great, but there's something about taking advantage of a woman that never sat well with me. I just wasn't that kind of guy. And, no, it didn't matter that she'd originally been intent on ending my life, either. It was the principle of the thing.

"Then you'll tell me anything I want to know?"

"Hardly," she replied. "I just meant that you could do anything you wanted to me in a sexual fashion." She winked. "Maybe a little *Fifty Furs of Gray* action?"

"What?"

"Never mind." She slithered up next to me. "So, what can I do for you...Master?"

"I...uh..."

"I'm very good at certain things," she whispered while licking her lips.

"But...your teeth."

She stood back for a moment and closed her eyes. It took longer than I would have expected, but within about thirty seconds she was back to full human.

"So you *could* have gone full wolf," I stated, keeping Boomy at the ready. I wasn't used to that being a possibility after I'd unleashed my energy into a werewolf. "Interesting."

"Ah, you'd rather I do that before we get frisky?"

"What?" I said, grimacing. "No! I just meant that you would have been able to fight me better that way."

Her eyes ran over my body.

"Why would I want to fight you, lover?"

Gulp.

The Admiral, which was the name Rachel had given to

Little Ian, was starting to wake up. Again, this chick in human form was smokin' hot.

But I couldn't allow that. Still, I had to play this chick.

"Okay," I said, tucking away Boomy. "So you want to play, do you?"

"Mmmm-hmmm."

"Turn around, then."

She complied without hesitation.

I whipped out a pair of handcuffs and cinched them around her wrists. She cooed in response.

Leaning in, I whispered, "Where is Rachel Cress?"

"I can't tell you that."

I sent a wave of energy through her. She jolted and yelped.

"Where is Rachel Cress?"

"I…" She swallowed hard. "I…can't…"

Another wave dropped her to the ground, leaving her convulsing with pleasure. She was writhing and moaning.

Then I knelt beside her and began to reach out again.

This time I stopped.

Her eyes looked longingly at my hand.

"Please," she hissed.

I raised an eyebrow. "Where is Rachel Cress?"

"I can't tell you."

"The next touch I give you," I said in a whisper, "will take you to a level of bliss you've never even imagined."

"Yes, yes, please."

"All you have to do is tell me what I want to know and I'll rock your world."

The look on her face was a mixture of hate, lust, betrayal, and desire. It was obvious that she was damn close to losing her mind, and it was also clear that she understood what was really at stake here.

"You promise you won't just leave me here in agony?"

I reached out, hovering my hand just above her thigh.

"You've my word."

"Temple Church," she blurted like a woman possessed. "Now touch me, you sexy bastard!"

"Wait," I said, keeping her at bay. "Before I do that, I must first remove what I did to you. If you still want me after that, I'll comply."

I then removed all the amalgamite sexual energy from her until the lust in her eyes dissipated.

She was back to normal.

"Still interested?" I asked with a raised eyebrow.

Her response was less than excited, but she gave me another head-to-toe scan and said, "Only if you do that tingly spell on me again," she said with a shrug.

"Right."

CHAPTER 17

"*L*et's go," I said as I walked by Harvey and Leland, both looking relaxed from their meals.

I didn't know precisely where this Temple Church was, but I was pretty certain it wasn't inside The Chandos.

My fellow officers walked out a few moments later and I detailed that I had the information we needed in order to find Rachel. I also handed back Harvey's magnifying glass, though I had to admit that it had come in handy.

Leland was rubbing his chin in James Bond fashion. "Temple Church is rather a journey from here on foot, but we can either grab a car or take the Tube."

"It doesn't matter to me how we get there," I said, "as long as we get there."

Leland nodded and began walking back toward the monument where I'd found Rachel's glove. I now had her badge in my pocket as well. Pretty soon, I hoped to collect everything about her, though hopefully in one piece.

"How do you know she's at that church, Chief?" Harvey asked as we followed after Leland. "Was there a document or something that you found?"

"Let's just say that I gave a doggy a bone, and leave it at that."

"That sounds kind of creepy, Chief."

I replayed what I'd just said over in my head and, sure enough, it *did* sound creepy.

"Right, well, I played a game and won."

"The challenge game that the werewolf guy was talking about?"

"No, not that one. A different one."

"I don't get it."

I didn't bother to try and explain. Leland was moving at breakneck speed now and I didn't want to lose him. It was almost as if he'd suddenly picked up the trail of something with his nose.

We ran down the steps and across Trafalgar Square until we got to a sign that said "Underground" on it. It was on a white-and-red circle.

"Charing Cross," announced Leland while motioning at the sign. "Or we can catch a cab."

"Again, Leland," I replied, "whichever is easiest."

"Right." He rubbed his chin again as his forehead creased. "Seeing that our badges will let us through the turnstiles without pause, I'd say we should take the Tube."

"Fine."

"Uh, Chief?" said Harvey with a look of worry.

"Yes?"

It was clear he didn't want to say what he was about to say, but finally he announced, "I don't like the subway."

"Why not?"

"It's…" He leaned over and stared down the stairs that led underground. "It's under the city. Who knows if all this stuff might fall on us or not?"

I furrowed my brow at him. "You jumped into a null zone and fought werewolves without a problem, Harvey."

"I know, but this is different."

"I can't see—" I stopped myself. "Honestly, we don't have time for this. If you'd prefer a taxi, we'll do that. I don't care. We just have to go."

"No, no," he said, looking to be hardening his resolve. "I can do this. I'm a cop, right?"

"Well…"

"And cops have to face their fears, right?"

I held my reply and instead crossed my arms and tapped my foot.

"You *can* do this, Harvey," Leland said assuringly. "I have faith in you, old boy!"

"Yeah?"

"Indubitably."

"Okay," Harvey replied after a moment. "Thanks, Leland. You're a real pal."

They both started to walk down the stairs into the Underground as I stood there perplexed.

"Leland," I called out, "seeing that there is a portal hub at St. Martin-in-the-Fields, would there also be one at the other churches?"

He stopped.

"Not in every church, no, but quite of few of them do have them."

"Temple Church, maybe?"

He reached into his jacket, pulled out a map, and began studying it.

I rolled my eyes.

"Lydia," I said through the connector, "is there a portal in Temple Church?"

"There sure is, honeycakes."

"Thanks, baby."

"Everything okay?"

"We'll see," I replied. "Can't talk right now, I'm afraid."

"Oh." She sounded pouty. "Keep me posted, okay?"

"I will." I clicked off the connection and said, "There is one" at the same time that Leland's eyes grew excited and he stabbed a finger at his map.

He looked up.

"How did you know?"

"Lydia, our AI. I just asked her."

"Ah," he said sourly as he folded up his map and stuffed it back into his suit. "The older ways are just as valid, you know."

Harvey's face was looking rather hopeful. His eyes darted back and forth between me and Leland.

"Does this mean we don't have to go through the subway?"

"That's right," I answered as I started a brisk walk back toward St. Martins-in-the-Fields. "We're going to jump right into their back yard."

They'd never expect that.

CHAPTER 18

*T*urns out they were expecting us. There was a welcome party and everything.

Swell.

Standing before us were a bunch of wolves, all in full form and all in different shapes and sizes. While I'm sure that Leland and Harvey had their eyes on the larger, more muscular ones, I focused my attention on the smaller dogs. They had a tendency to be more vicious.

"I didn't know the London Dog Show was in town," I stated.

It was always best to irritate werewolves when you were about to fight them. They got reckless when they were angry.

To prove my point, one of them growled and started toward me. Another grabbed that one and threw him back.

This caused a small fight to break out among them,

but it was quickly squashed when a massive growl sounded from the back of the room.

I didn't like that sound.

Not even a little bit.

"Uh, Chief," whispered Harvey, "what was that?"

"Your guess is as good as mine."

"Commence the challenge," demanded a booming voice that clearly had belonged to the same creature who released that growl.

The wolves all backed away and a single female wolf approached us.

I pulled out Boomy.

"Sorry, Mr. Dex," she said, holding out her hand, "but there are no weapons allowed in the arena."

"Huh?"

That's when I looked around more carefully.

Shit.

We were indeed standing in the pit of an arena. It wasn't anything like the one that the valkyries had in the nine levels, but it was definitely a place intended for fighting.

And in a church, no less!

Maybe they used it during the Crusades back in the day? What a way to go. I guess, from their perspective, it was a quicker trip to the afterlife from here. Something told me that our new pal Reaper might disagree with that sentiment.

"Please don't make us take your weapons by force, Mr. Dex," she said in a tight growl. "It would be such a shame for you to perish before you begin."

I glanced around at all the drooling faces. One on one I had a chance. All of them at once would be impossible.

Going against everything in my being, I handed over Boomy.

"Take care of it," I warned her. "I plan on having it back when this is all said and done."

Her lip came up in either a snarl or a smile. It was hard to tell the difference with doggies.

"I applaud your confidence," she said as she took the weapons from Harvey and Leland.

Then she snapped her fingers and a number of wolves came over to seize my partners.

"Hey," I said, "what's going on?"

"They're being taken out of the equation," she answered. "If you win, they'll live; if not…well, tsk-tsk."

"Chief?" Harvey said, looking ready to struggle.

I shook my head at him.

This was all on me. If he put up a fight, they'd just use him as an example of what they'd do to Leland next.

I watched as the wolves took Harvey and Leland over to a wall, up a flight of stairs and then plopped them down in a couple of seats. After chaining them up, the wolf who had taken our weapons moved to the center of the ring.

"Wolves, hear me," she said in dramatic fashion. "This is the famous Ian Dex."

Famous? I mean, sure, I was a hit with the ladies, but…

"He is an amalgamite. An abomination."

Why did everyone consider me an abomination? Granted, I preferred being called that over being mistaken for a vampire, but it was still kind of hurtful.

The wolves were growling sinisterly at me.

As if they were any better.

"The tournament shall now begin!"

The howls that filled the room made me cringe. I covered my ears until they calmed down.

"Uh, excuse me," I said, holding up my hand.

"Yes?" said the apparent master of ceremonies.

"I get that I'm supposed to be fighting in a tournament and all of that, but could I at least get an idea for what the rules are and such?"

The wolves all chuckled.

"There are no rules, Mr. Dex."

"Great," I replied while rubbing my hands, "I'd like my gun back, then."

The chuckling stopped.

"Okay, there is one rule," she stated as her eyes creased.

"Figures. Now, do we fight to the death or what?"

"Yes."

"Any exceptions to that?"

"No."

I nodded. "So that makes it two rules, yes?"

She licked her chops. "I suppose so, but that one was pretty much just common sense."

Anything I could do to get them off their game would only prove to help me when the actual fighting started.

"And will I be fighting everyone at once?"

"Of course not," she answered as though I were stupid. "How would that be fair?"

"'One at a time' is rule number three, it seems," I said, wearing my best shit-eating grin. "I'd say there are a lot more rules than you'd originally let on to, Puddles."

She snapped back as if slapped. "Puddles?"

"Sorry, I don't know your real name." I then leaned to the side and looked her up and down with a bit of dramatic flair. "But looking at you, I'd imagine you've stained more than one carpet in your time."

The wolves chuckled again.

"Silence!" she screamed.

Surprisingly, they complied. Did that mean she was the current leader? If so, why was she allowing this challenge to happen? Maybe she didn't have a choice? Wolves were an interesting bunch. I thought back to the horrendous growl from earlier. Clearly that hadn't come from her, so that meant she was only close to the top.

"My name is Marissa," she snarled, "thank you very much."

"Ah, my apologies," I said with a bow. "Now, will I have time to recover between bouts?"

"No."

"I see." I scanned all the hungry faces. "That means whoever goes first will be the only one who actually gets a real challenge. After that, each one I fight will find the battle successively easier until I'm so tired that the one who wins against me will do so not out of strength but out of luck."

"Luck?"

"Sure." I shrugged at her. "It's not difficult to win a battle against someone who is too exhausted to put up a fight. So, that means the doggie who finally whoops me will have been fortunate in that he or she didn't have to face me when I was at full stamina."

Their faces were all confused now.

Obviously they could understand that I'd had a point. If their real purpose in this battle was to test their mettle, they'd need to do so with me being at my best. To do anything else wouldn't test their strength at all.

"You have a point," affirmed Marissa, "and therefore I declare that you will only be facing our top three fighters."

The doggies began to whine, but they stopped the instant Marissa glared at them.

She definitely had *some* control over this clan.

"Great." I beamed. "That means that only the third guy is the lucky one. I'm not sure who that will be," I added more loudly, "but good for you in beating someone who isn't functioning at his full potential. You'll definitely feel proud about that, no doubt."

Just as Marissa was about to respond to my statement, the sound of clapping hands filled the room. It was an ominous clap. The kind of clap you heard when someone was being incredibly sarcastic. And it was loud, sounding like it was coming via the hands of a giant.

"I like you, Dex," said the same voice that had sounded earlier. The one that belonged to that original growl. "You're a real asshole."

I fought to adjust my vision so I could see through the darkness and toward the source of the voice, but it was more than just an absence of light, it was a shroud of some sort.

"Thanks," I answered back. "I guess."

"Marissa, the man is correct in his assessment."

"As you say, my lord," she demurred, dropping to a knee.

"And I would not wish to fight him in any way that would not give *me* his best, either."

Him?

Marissa's muzzle came up at that announcement, too. "What are you saying, my lord?"

"That I shall be the only one who fights him on this day," Captain Loudmouth concluded.

The wolves were a mix of terror and disappointment, but it was clear that nobody was going to say anything about it.

"But—"

"Are you challenging my command, Marissa?" queried the apparent alpha dog, as if he were expecting her to fold.

She lowered to a second knee. "Never, my lord."

"Good. Now, clear the arena and move everyone to the stands."

He pulled away the shroud that had been blocking my vision and stood up. Then he jumped from the balcony and landed in the opposite side of the arena from me.

This was no Chihuahua.

He was easily eight feet tall, muscular as hell, and had teeth that I felt certain could penetrate my skin without much fuss.

I know that I was all about looking out for the little wolves earlier, but this guy had my full attention now.

"Chief?" implored Harvey in desperation as a number of wolves held him back.

"No," I commanded through the connector as I bore deeper into the shadows on the upper level, hoping to spot Rachel. She wasn't there. "Control yourself, Harvey.

Don't go into werebear mode unless you have to. If I don't make it out of this alive, it'll be on you to get Rachel and Leland out of here."

"That guy's huge, though, Chief."

"The bigger they are, the harder they fall, right?"

"If you say so," he replied, "but if that guy falls on you, you're dead."

I wanted to thank him for the vote of confidence, but the fact was that he was right.

This dude was massive.

I'd need to employ some tricks if I was going to have a chance of winning against the likes of him.

"Now, Mr. Dex..." he began.

"Do you have a name?" I interrupted, trying to get the upper hand. "Or should I just call you Rex?"

He groaned and looked around at everyone.

"Okay, who told him my name?" he ranted. "I was very clear that I was going to introduce myself, wasn't I?" Rex turned back to me, shaking his head. "It's so hard to find good help these days, you know?"

"Uh, yeah, actually," I answered, fighting not to look in Harvey's direction, "but nobody told me your name. I just guessed."

"Oh." He stood back up. "Sorry, everyone. My bad."

"Anyway," I spoke up quickly, "the same goes for you that goes for the others who wanted to challenge me, you know?"

He tilted his head like a dog who had just heard a funny sound.

"What do you mean?"

"You're huge." I laughed while motioning at him. "It's

not a fair fight. All you're really going to be proving by ripping me to shreds is that you can tear apart someone who isn't anywhere near your strength and size."

He chuckled like the other dogs had earlier. Then he began walking around the arena slowly.

"I'm no fool, Mr. Dex," he said. "I know that you have many skills at your disposal."

"Then you should also know that I can't just turn them on in an instant. They take time for me to prepare, they don't last forever, and they exhaust me in the process."

"Fair enough," Rex stated as he continued his pacing. "Here is what I suggest: You should carefully choose which of your skills to use in this battle. I will give you time to activate said skill. If you and I are still standing when the round is over, I will provide you with an elixir to rebuild your strength to full and will allow you to choose another skill."

Was this guy being legit? And *rounds*? What was this, some kind of boxing match?

"Seriously?" I said finally.

"Of course," he answered with his hands out. "I've no wish to destroy you unless you are at your best, for you are correct in that it would prove nothing."

"Well, okay then."

Then he stopped and gave me a hard stare.

"I expect your best, Mr. Dex," he pointed out. "Anything less will make the death of your friends very unpleasant indeed."

"Fine," I said, recognizing that I probably wasn't going to survive. The least I could do was give a quick death to the others with me.

"Good," he answered with a nod. "Now, if you look straight up, you will find your lovely Rachel Cress as well."

There she was, in a cage that was hanging over the arena.

She was staring down at me with angry eyes.

"Rachel," I stammered.

"Idiot," she replied.

CHAPTER 19

*W*ell, that was gratitude for you. Here I was coming all the way to London, leaving my Vegas crew behind so I could help my former partner get free from the binds of a bunch of werewolves, and she was calling me an idiot.

"What the hell?" I said.

"You're a moron," she declared. "This entire thing has been a trap to get you here."

"Obviously."

"And yet you did it anyway?"

"You're my partner, Rachel."

"Ex-partner," Leland started loudly, but he significantly quieted as all the wolves turned to look at him. "Sorry."

"And what good is that going to do me when this guy comes at you?" She spat as she pointed at Rex. "I've seen his *speed*, Ian. You can't match his *speed*."

She was clearly homing in on that word.

"He's fast, eh?" I sought to clarify.

"Very," she answered. "You'll have to move with *Haste* to even have a chance at him."

"I got it, I got it," I said through the connector, thinking that it would make more sense to speak with her in private. It was dead, though.

"Rachel, you there?"

Nothing.

Great, they'd somehow made it impossible for me to talk with her. I knew my connector was fine because I'd been speaking with Harvey, but I couldn't get through to Rachel.

Maybe I could use Harvey as a relay.

"Hey," I connected to him, "can you reach Rachel from where you are?"

"Sure." He then called out, "Hey, Rachel, it's me, Harvey!"

"Uh...hi," she said in response.

"I'm talking about through your connector, Harvey," I groaned.

"Oh, sorry." A moment later he added, "Nah, it's dead. I got an idea, though. One second."

I began stretching as Rex did the same.

"Just checked with Leland and Lydia, Chief. Nobody can get to her."

"Damn it," I replied. "All right. Well, while I'm fighting this guy, do your best to come up with something to get you guys out of here."

"Like what?"

I glared at him. "How the hell do I know? Just think, will you?"

"Right, right. Sorry, Chief."

Here I was about to have my body torn in two by the biggest werewolf known to man, and Harvey was asking me to brainstorm with him regarding ideas on how to get out of this mess.

"You have one minute to prepare, Mr. Dex," Rex stated as he walked back to his side of the ring. "Do choose your skill carefully. I would truly hate for this to be too simple of a fight."

I didn't reply.

There was no point.

Rachel had given me a hint. I would go with what she'd suggested. She'd been around him a lot more than I had, after all.

I calmed my mind as best as I could and slowed my breathing.

Rachel had suggested I employ *Haste*, so that's what I was going to do.

If I made it out of this round, I'd have to choose something else next. I couldn't use any skill in succession, not without quite a delay between them anyway, so I'd have to pick wisely.

Time, my mind said.

That was probably going to be one I'd have to use. *Flashes*, too, no doubt.

But I had to be careful because I only had one *Time* left. Of course, using it was better than dying.

The one good thing about those particular spells, or

skills—or whatever the hell they were, was that they didn't take anything but a stated thought to launch them. They made me a little wobbly, of course, except for *Sniff*, but I really saw no need to employ that one at the moment.

I focused again until *Haste* took over.

It was time to fight.

CHAPTER 20

Haste was engaged and I was ready to fight, but I learned real quick that Rachel was correct in her assessment regarding Rex the uberwolf.

This dude made *Haste* nothing but an even playing field.

He smiled in his wolfish way.

"I know about your various skills, Mr. Dex," he gloated, "and I fully expected that your first selection would be *Haste*."

Fighting to get the upper hand, I replied, "Well, Rachel *did* just suggest it pretty heavily."

"Ah," he said, inclining his head, "I was wondering why she was speaking certain words with so much emphasis."

I glanced up at Rachel to see a slow smirk forming on her face. I thought the word "idiot" for her.

"Okay, so we're the same speed now and I have no weapons."

"Very astute observation, Mr. Dex."

"Still not much of a fair fight then, is it?" I said, seeking to make him question the validity of this battle.

He moved in closer and we began to circle around each other. I was seeking out weak points on his person, but I couldn't spot anything obvious. The dude was just a brick wall of muscle and fangs.

"I'll let you in on a little secret," he whispered menacingly. "You have no chance of beating me even if all things were even. I'm merely leveling the playing field as best as I can so that my flock will be pleased."

"Kind of cowardly for a wolf, no?"

His eye twitched. "What would you have me do, Mr. Dex, tie one arm behind my back?"

"It's a start."

"And you'd still be no match for me." He gripped and released his hands a few times. "The fact is that *nobody* can match my ability."

"Sure are confident in yourself."

"Supremely," he affirmed. "Now, what say we get on with this charade?"

My adrenaline was on the rise, *Haste* was engaged, and my pants were preparing to be filled with shit. This made the nine levels feel like a trip to Disney World.

"Okidoki," I said casually, "but one last thing?"

He rolled his eyes. "Go on."

"Your second in command," I said, pointing behind him, "is she supposed to be pointing a gun at you?"

"What?"

The moment he spun, I leaped onto his back and got

him in a rear naked choke, wrapping my legs around his chest and locking my ankles.

He grabbed at my arms to try and free himself, but it was abundantly obvious that he wasn't prepared for the level of strength I had as an amalgamite.

I squeezed as hard as I could.

Using a line from a poem I'd recently heard, I hollered, "Die, fucker, die!"

Unfortunately, Rex had other plans.

He must have recognized that there was no easy way out of this and so he grabbed my ankles instead of my arms, dislodging their connection to each other. I tried to swing them back together, but by now he had yanked one of my free legs so hard that I thought certain it was going to pull right out of my hip joint.

I grunted and released my kung-fu grip.

"Fuck," I said as I landed on the ground and rolled away, jumping back to my feet with a wobble.

My right leg was tingling, but it'd heal soon enough.

Rex, on the other hand, was grabbing at his throat and choking.

There was no time to waste.

I took a page out of a Jean-Claude Van Damme movie and jumped up with a spinning kick. My leg was still tingling, but I didn't need it to be one hundred percent to do its job.

My foot tagged Rex right on the cheek and he stumbled backward.

It felt like I had just kicked granite.

He stopped, shook his head for a moment, and then spit out a fang.

Even if I died right here, at least I'd go knowing that he'd be dealing with some major dental work due to fighting me.

I backed away.

Far away.

He glared at me angrily for a few moments as rage welled up in his red eyes.

Then, with a massive roar, Rex flexed every muscle in his body and charged.

"Fuck, fuck, fuck," was all I could say before he launched himself at me.

If I hadn't had *Haste* engaged, I would have ended up being torn in half by the speed at which he was flying. His mass alone would have ended me. As it was, I was able to fall straight down and let him sail directly overhead.

Mostly.

His massive paw, hand, or whatever the hell it was, reached out just in time to knock the living shit out of me.

I've never been hit so hard in my life.

Seriously, I was even hearing the chirping of little birds.

But this was no time for pain or concussions—assuming I wanted to live, anyway. The way I was feeling, that would have taken a little contemplation, so I just went with wanting to live and moved on with things.

I got back to my feet and spun back to see two Rexes standing there.

It took me a second to realize that this was just because my vision was seriously messed up from that hit.

"Wait, wait, wait," I said, holding up my hands. All four of them. "You have something in your fur."

"I'm not falling for that again, Mr. Dex," he replied as he pulled back his hand and swiped at me.

I ducked.

He swung again.

I ducked again.

He faked a swing.

I ducked.

He finished his swing, clipping my shoulder this time.

I flew.

He laughed heartily and then stalked over to where I'd landed.

My head was ringing, my leg was tingling, my vision was fighting to right itself, and now my shoulder throbbed like hell. And this was only the first round!

As he hovered over me and drooled his vileness on my suit, I had the feeling there wasn't going to be a second round.

"And now I will literally bite your head off," he said with a sinisterness that should have been reserved for demons, and maybe dragons. "Any last words?"

"Could you brush your teeth first?" I requested flatly. "Or at least use some mouthwash?"

His eyes narrowed and in a flash he pulled back, cracked opened his wide jaw, and lunged.

I closed my eyes and waited to feel the embrace of darkness.

Ding ding ding!

He stopped.

"Shit," he groaned, his teeth touching the sides of my skull.

I opened one eye as he pulled away.

"What?" I asked, barely able to talk.

He pushed himself back to full height. "Round's over, Mr. Dex. But in the next round, you die."

"Oh, that's good."

CHAPTER 21

True to his word, Rex waited for me to fully recover, which included some kind of elixir that brought me back to full health and power.

My body was no longer aching and my vision was clear. I still had a bit of a headache, but something told me that was going to be there for a while. Rex had quite a wallop, after all.

"Any ideas?" I called up to Rachel in as quiet a voice as I could manage.

"Why are you trying to keep quiet?"

"Because I don't want him to hear us," I answered. "Duh."

"Seeing as how you told him that I was coaching you before," she chided, "it's not like he'll be surprised by anything I say."

"True." I then played back the words Rex had said to me while we were facing each other before the last round got underway. "He apparently knows everything about me anyway."

"Why don't you just get the hell out of here?" she suggested. "You know I hate playing the part of damsel in distress. It's such a misogynistic view of women." She crossed her arms in standard Rachel fashion. "I don't need some damn man to fight my battles."

I knew how she felt about such things, and she was right to feel the way she did. But this situation was different than she was playing it out to be. The wolves didn't kidnap her because they were trying to do the old "prince saving the princess" bit. They wanted to get to me no matter what. If Rachel's name had been Irving, and she'd been a six-foot-four vampire who was covered in tattoos and body piercings, they still would have stuck his ass in that cage to use as bait.

But Rachel wouldn't see it that way, no matter how I tried to position it.

"Would you rather be down here fighting him while I was up there in the cage?" I asked pointedly.

"Yes."

I should have expected that.

"Well, me too," I concurred, though that wasn't really true, "but that's not how it is, so deal with it."

"Then just let me die."

Knowing Rachel, she meant it. Her pride was worth quite a bit more to her than her life. I didn't know if that stubbornness was a Cress family trait or not, but I found it less than beneficial at times.

"And Harvey and Leland, too?" I said with accusing eyes. "You're all right with that, also?"

She cursed under her breath. "Nobody asked you to bring them here."

That was true, and frankly I would have been much happier during this entire mission if I'd not brought them along. So far they'd done little but get in my way, test my every last nerve, and pal around like a couple of long-lost friends.

"Look," I said firmly, "I'm not going to leave, so you either help me out or all four of us die."

The angst on her face was monumental.

I missed seeing that look.

"Use *Time*," she mouthed, keeping her face taut.

"But I only have one more use of that."

"So?"

"Isn't it obvious?" I said, blinking. "What if we need it at some point in the future?"

In response, Rachel pointed across the ring at Rex the uberwolf. Then she raised her eyebrows in an "are you fucking kidding me?" fashion.

She was right, of course, but...

"Do you have *any* other suggestions?" I pleaded.

"Suicide?"

"Wait," I said as a smile grew on my face. "You said you'd rather be down here fighting than me doing it, right?"

She squinted. "Yes."

"Then let's go with that."

"Slight problem with that plan, Einstein," she said in a rather pedantic tone. "I'm not sure if you've noticed or not, but I'm kind of stuck in a cage hanging over the arena."

It was my turn to point out *her* stupidity. Thoese moments were rare, so I quite relished them.

"Not if I *Channel* you."

Her look changed from sour to impressed. So you know, that, too, was a rarity.

I hadn't used *Channel* in a long time. It was one of the first skills I'd discovered. The problem with it was that not many people liked having themselves channeled through me. But in this instance, there wasn't much choice.

"It's a solid idea," she stated with a nod, "but the only way you can do that is if we touch or if you can get through to my connector."

"Damn it," I said. "Forgot about that."

"But it gives me an idea," she said as she tapped on the metal bar of her cage. "You could use Harvey's strength, if he'll let you."

A slow smile crept upon my face as I began to nod.

It wouldn't be nearly as effective as using Rachel's magical capabilities, but it'd make me easily double as strong as I was normally. There was still the problem of dealing with Rex's speed, since *Haste* was out of the picture now.

Still, it was better than nothing.

"Harvey," I said through the connector as I closed my eyes, "I'm going to need to channel your strength in order to fight in round two. Are you cool with that?"

"Do whatever you gotta do, Chief," he answered. "We all die if you lose anyway, right?"

"Yes."

"One question, though," he asked with a voice that seemed to quiver, "is it gonna hurt?"

"Only if he hits me or bites me or whatever."

"Huh?"

"I'm not just channeling your strength, Harvey," I said, "it'll be like we've merged."

"That sounds creepy."

"It's not a sexual thing, you weirdo."

"I never said it was, Chief," he commented. "I just meant that it was creepy because we'd be occupying the same head."

"Ah, sorry." I coughed. "Anyway, you'll be in my head as a bystander. You won't have any control, but you'll feel what I feel and I'll have access to all of your strength in addition to my own."

I glanced over at him and he nodded, but he didn't look like he was all that interested in playing. To his point, though, it was either this or certain death. At least this would give us all a chance at round three.

"And you have to keep silent, no matter how bad it hurts."

"Why?"

"Because we can't let him know that I'm using your strength or he'll just destroy me with speed."

"Got it, Chief," Harvey agreed stoically. "I'm ready."

I closed my eyes and reached out.

CHAPTER 22

I stood across the arena from Rex as I felt the power of a full werebear adding in to my amalgamite strength.

"Question," I yelled out, making sure all the wolves could hear me. "Is it fair that you have superior speed to me? I know how important it is for everyone here to see an even battle."

"Superior speed is merely part of who I am, Mr. Dex," he countered. "All wolves are faster than humans, as you know."

"Stronger, too," I replied. "But we're not talking about standard wolf-speed here, Rex. We're talking about the level of speed that you know is far beyond anything normal."

"So?"

I shrugged. "Hey, if you want to cheat your way to victory, that's your call. I just thought that werewolves were an honorable sort." I did a quick scan of the arena. "I guess I heard that wrong."

Rex stood there for a moment, taking in what I'd just said to his flock. He was a wolf who had a decision to make. It was one thing to flaunt your power to non-wolves, but his followers weren't going to be all that forgiving if they felt he was winning unfairly. It *was* fair that he use every asset available to him, of course. I was completely aware of that. Hell, if I had Boomy in my hand, I'd have unloaded a flurry of breaker bullets into Rex's head by now. But that wasn't the point. These were wolves. They had a code, at least when it came to challenges, and this *was* a challenge game, right?

"No," Rex said finally, "you were not wrong in your assessment of my race, Mr. Dex." He began walking forward. "However, you *are* wrong to assume that my use of my assets is against our moral code. We, as wolves, are superior to every race in every way. For me to squelch one of my skills in order to bring myself to your level would be the real break in honor, Mr. Dex, for I would not be giving you my full ability."

He'd used my own logic against me.

Smart.

"This is why I wished for you to utilize any of your particular skills, Mr. Dex." He raised his hands at the crowd. "You see, I *want* your best in this fight because it is the way of the wolf when in challenge mode. In return, I have no choice but to provide my best as well." His gaze was rather uppity as he said, "Do you understand, Mr. Dex, or shall I bring out some crayons and draw you a picture?"

The wolves chuckled.

"No need to be a dick about it, dude," I spat back. "Unless, of course, that's also one of your special skills?"

The wolves chuckled louder until Rex spun on them.

They silenced.

"It will be a pleasure to finally kill you, Mr. Dex," he breathed while closing the distance between us. "I only wish I could do so one thousand times instead of just once."

I held my reply as I prepared for his onslaught. While I knew there was no way I could keep up with his speed, I also had learned enough about the way he moved during the first round that I could make guesses. What I didn't want to do was give away my level of power until I had no choice. It would only take one interaction with my strength to let him know he'd have to keep his distance while picking me apart piece by piece.

There was no way he was going to fall for any more of my tricks either. He'd proved that when I tried for the old "you've got something on your fur" routine.

Too bad I didn't have any tennis balls on my person. Maybe he'd be up for a game of fetch.

I nearly laughed at the thought.

So that left me with the only option I had. Get the hell beat out of me while hoping I could get my hands on Rex in such a way that I could end him.

Oh, and I had to stay away from those damn teeth of his, too.

"Fine," I said, readying myself for some serious punishment. "Why don't we quit talking about it and get to it?"

In response, he smiled in his doggish way, cracked his jaw, and headed back to his side of the ring.

Great. He was planning to really make a show of this for his crowd of admirers.

I, too, backed away and got myself as close to the arena wall as possible. If nothing else, he'd have to attack me from the front. I knew how fast *Haste* allowed me to move, and since his speed matched mine when I was using that skill, I also understood what I needed to do to cut down on his options.

"Kill him, Ian," Rachel shouted from her perch above the action. "Rip his fucking throat out."

That was definitely an option with my newfound strength.

I nodded at her as our eyes locked for a moment.

In all my years, I'd never met anyone quite like Rachel. Tough, independent, gorgeous, and willing to call me on my shit at the drop of a hat. Yes, I'd bedded down with more women than Hugh Hefner, but they were all just lustful excursions. Sure, I really liked a lot of the ladies I'd been with, such as Serena and Paula, but nobody was like Rachel. Nobody.

But now wasn't the time to get all sentimental.

There was a massive wolf standing across from me who was harboring some seriously nefarious intentions toward me.

If my head wasn't in the game, there'd be no future for any of us.

I tore my eyes away from Rachel and steeled my nerves. If Rex thought this was going to be easy, he was in for quite a surprise.

"Get ready, Harvey," I said through the connector, "here comes the pain."

My werebear partner merely whimpered in response.

CHAPTER 23

The blur known as Rex came zooming across the arena. I barely even had time to lift my arms in the hopes of blocking the initial strike.

I failed.

He clubbed me right in the chest with such a ferocious blow that I thought certain there'd be a hole when I looked down. My back slammed against the wall, too. There was no give. It was like a lumberjack taking a sledgehammer and crushing it into you at full power while you were flat against concrete.

"Owwwwwww," came the booming yell of Harvey the werebear.

It was so loud that everything stopped.

The crowd ceased its cheering.

Rex slowed to a crawl and looked over at where Harvey sat.

Even the pain I was feeling seemed a distant ache as

my brain struggled to think of the words I could use through the connector at him.

Fortunately, he recovered.

"Uh," he said, "*that* looked really painful."

You could have heard a pin drop, and this was a dirt floor. "I've seen a lot of, uh, mixed martial arts fights in my day, but that was…" He held out a congratulatory thumbs-up with a wince. "That was just…wow."

"Thank you," Rex replied with a confused look.

While I wanted to borrow Rachel's line and call Harvey an idiot, he'd inadvertently helped my situation.

Again, Rex had slowed to a crawl.

I took advantage of the opportunity and locked on to both of his wrists. Then, I squeezed.

His muzzle spun toward me and he shook his arms fiercely in an effort to get away.

No dice.

He growled and snapped at me, but I just pushed him out farther. He went into a blur while spinning and turning and pulling, but the combination of my amalgamite strength and Harvey's werebear power must have made it feel like Rex had irons on his wrists.

Finally, he stopped and leveled his eyes at me.

"Clever," he said, panting. "I must admit that I hadn't expected you to use the werebear against me. But it's still only a matter of time before I tear you to shreds."

With that, he leaped up and tried to kick me.

Now, if you've ever danced with a dog by grabbing their front paws and prancing around a bit in dancing fashion, you'll know that they have very little ability to use their hind legs. You'd expect that this would be different with a werewolf. Turns out, not so much.

"You look ridiculous," I said as the wolves in the crowd began howling with laughter. "Seems like your adoring flock agrees with me as well."

His eyes began glowing red.

I didn't know exactly what this meant, but I couldn't imagine it would be good.

Then he bared his teeth, completing the incredibly creepy visual. His breath didn't help the vibe either.

And that's when the word *Flashes* hit me.

Now, unlike the other little fun games that Gabe the vampire had hooked me up with, *Flashes* wasn't something I could control. Or, if it was, I had no idea how to do it. *Flashes* just seemed to trigger when it wanted to. The first time it'd happened was when I'd bumped into Shitfaced Fred on the old Strip. The second time was when a chunk of Charlotte the dragon's flesh landed on me in Blood Bane Tower. This time, though, it seemed that Rex had to get riled up enough to trigger the event.

The world froze.

CHAPTER 24

*J*ust like the other two times *Flashes* kicked off, I found myself looking through the eyes of a mystery person. I never knew who it was or if it was even the same set of eyes every time. It *felt* the same, but that was probably because it was *me* living through it.

I was standing outside of a building in downtown Vegas. I recognized the place, but I couldn't remember the details of it. There was a haze around my memory of it, almost like what happened whenever I caught sight of one of the Directors.

There was a side door that led down a flight of stairs. I'd kind of hoped we'd be going through a main glass entrance so I could catch a reflection of who I was floating around inside.

Maybe next time.

At the bottom of the stairs was a hidden zone. This was similar to a null zone, but it was further masked with runes so that not even supernaturals could find it...unless they knew where to look.

The area lit up for a moment and I saw a portal open.

It wasn't the standard portal I was used to. This one looked more like a black door-sized void that didn't so much jump from one dimension to another, but rather just acted as a regular, well, door.

The person I was inhabiting stepped inside and walked across a room that had various industrial vats running along the walls. I couldn't see anything in any of them, though, because they were all made of metal. The center of the room had various tubes, beakers, and computers. It reminded me of my chemistry classes back in high school, but on a much larger scale.

We walked through another doorway that led down into a dark dungeon-like cavern.

Seated in the middle of the room was Rex. I recognized him immediately because of the red circle of fur that was on his right shoulder. It looked like a bullseye.

He stared back at whomever it was that I was inhabiting and nodded a few times. Obviously, my ride was speaking to him, but I couldn't hear anything being said.

Rex's eyes weren't the glowing red I'd seen before. They were blurry and dazed, and he looked majorly out of it.

He was either in a trance or he was drugged.

Either way, it wasn't the same level of Rex I was dealing with in the arena.

Another person came into the room.

This was more a sensation than a visual, though, because I couldn't see this person. I just knew that… she?…was there.

As if confirming my suspicions, Rex turned a weary head toward her and then jumped to his feet, a howl releasing from his lips as anger filled his face.

The scene suddenly changed.

I was no longer in the dungeon or whatever it was. Now, I was standing in a forest somewhere that I couldn't place. If I had to guess, I would have said somewhere in Washington state or maybe even Canada.

The body I was in began to float up until we were looking down at the clearing. Magic? Was I in a mage of some sort?

From the side of the clearing walked a small wolf that had a red circle on its shoulder.

Was this Rex, but younger?

A set of other wolves slowly closed in on him.

It looked like my pal Rex was about to be ambushed.

I couldn't help but think he deserved it. Then again, it was clear that he'd gotten out of this fight alive or I wouldn't be standing in an arena with him in the real world.

So, what was the point of this vision?

One thing I'd learned from *Flashes* thus far was that they always had a point—some means of allowing me to defeat the bad guy or maybe an indication of how I could escape a critical situation. Yes, I'd only had two episodes before this one, but both were beneficial to me in some way.

The wolves dived at him.

He jumped to the side and tore the throat from the one closest to him. The instant the dead wolf hit the ground, Rex grew slightly and a flash of light surrounded him. This made the next wolf to hit him die even faster than the first.

With each successive death came greater power for Rex.

Greater size.

Greater ferocity.

Could that be the message here? If Rex killed me, he'd get my strength and abilities? If so, it was even worse because he'd also be getting Harvey's power.

After a few wolves had met the maker, though, Rex's size increases stopped.

So there *was* a limit.

That was good, at least, and it made sense. If there had been no limit, he could have just gone and hunted down supernaturals and killed them all until he was the most powerful beast to ever walk the earth.

But that was it, wasn't it? He needed me because I was unique. He'd probably killed every other type of supernatural out there, inheriting their skills and abilities.

He was essentially the wolf version of me.

Rex was an amalgamite in wolf's clothing.

Shit.

lashes stopped, leaving me dazed and a bit confused, but I refused to let that hinder my grip on Rex's wrists.

In his world, not even a second had elapsed, but his eyes settled on me and he squinted. It was like he knew that I knew.

He snarled and snapped his teeth at my arm, but I spun and lifted him up, smacking his back against the wall I'd been pressed up against moments before.

Then, with a feeling of menace that I'd not felt in quite some time, I went berserk.

Maybe it was the rush of power in my body or maybe it was the fact that this fucker was about to destroy me so he could soak in my power to add to his own, making me somehow part of this swath of destruction he was clearly intent on releasing on the world. I don't know, but I was feeling pretty pissed.

I swung him again and again against that wall, screaming with each hit.

He grunted and howled as the crowd sat in stunned silence.

From their perspective, I shouldn't have been able to manage doing what I was doing. Hell, from *my* perspective I shouldn't have been able to do what I was doing. If it wasn't for the fact that I'd called on *Channel* with Harvey, I'd be lying in a puddle of my own blood while Rex grew in power to proportions that were unfathomable.

And so I swung him around like a rag doll. I smashed him on the ground and on the walls of the arena.

I raged at him as he struggled to free himself. He could definitely take a lot of punishment.

Too bad for him that he had to die, before he could take me over.

Unfortunately, he had other plans.

In between crushing blows, his body began to warm. His wrists got so hot that they started burning my hands. I fought to stop the pain, but it was searing my flesh. I gritted my teeth as I held on for dear life.

It was getting impossible to stomach, though.

And while I could take a lot of pain, Harvey was clearly less capable of it. He screamed while holding up his hands and staring at them. There'd be no permanent damage on Harvey, and I'd heal within minutes, but it was simply too much for me to manage.

It was time to let go of Rex the uberwolf.

With a few spins, like I was in the discus event at the Olympics, I launched the wolf through the air with such fierceness that he could do nothing but wait until the impact of whatever stopped him struck.

Sadly for him, the thing that brought him to a halt was a pointed iron cross that was angled out of the wall. It pierced him through the neck, separating his head partially from his body.

He fell to the ground and lay still as I fell to my knees in exhaustion.

The wolves stared, with shock in their eyes, at the deceased form of their fallen leader.

There was a general murmuring that filled the air. It was as if they were all sharing shocked remarks about how I had destroyed their fearless leader. I couldn't blame them since I was equally shocked at this outcome. I was used to having a team helping me with these fights, after all.

But now what was going to happen?

Would the next wolf in line come down and seek glory through my death?

I kind of doubted that because none of them could have bested Rex, and I just had. Werwolves were territorial and they nearly always sought to become top dog, but they weren't typically insane about it. They knew when a fight was pointless.

Unfortunately, they also tended to be rather vengeful.

I'd just killed their leader, and while it was obvious I could dispatch each of them in single file, I couldn't stop a feeding frenzy.

The pain in my hands began to fade as I struggled to get to my feet. If I was going to face my doom, it'd be standing.

"Chief," Harvey said tiredly through the connector, "you did it."

"Don't get excited, Harvey," I replied. "I've got a feeling this isn't over yet."

"But—"

The wolves all stood and began walking down to the field with serious looks on their faces.

"Oh," finished Harvey.

The only sound that could be heard was that of footsteps and shuffling of dirt as the contingency of wolves began lining up in the arena.

"Ian?" Rachel rasped, looking as worried as I felt.

I glanced up at her.

"I don't know," I stated, knowing she was wondering if I had any idea what the doggies were up to.

At this point, I was barely able to keep my feet under me. I coughed and wheezed as my chest continued to heal from that original punch Rex landed at the beginning of the round.

I swallowed and glanced painfully back up at my ex-partner.

"Rachel, in the event that we've reached the end of our lives, I just want you to know that—"

"I know," she interrupted. "I know."

I nodded and then fell over as exhaustion overtook me and *Channel* dissipated.

Harvey's strength was no longer part of me.

Everything went black.

CHAPTER 26

J awoke to find that Rachel had been taken down and moved to be near Harvey and Leland. They were being flanked by wolves.

My chest was fully healed and my hands felt fine, but I still had a bit of a headache.

I'd live.

I glanced around again at all the muzzles in the room.

Maybe I'd live.

The master of ceremonies, Marissa, the wolf who had taken Boomy from me originally, stepped out and walked toward me. I didn't move, but I got myself ready for another fight. Fortunately, she wouldn't be nearly as difficult to end as Rex. The rest of the clan, though...well, that was a different matter altogether.

I looked around for a way out of this mess. Then I sighed. Even if I could find a way out, I wasn't going to bolt without my crew. Yes, that included Leland. While he wasn't a member of the Vegas PPD (thank the universe), he was still a fellow officer.

So I squared my shoulders and prepared for what I assumed would be round three.

"Mr. Dex," said the wolf approaching me, "you have succeeded in besting our leader."

I wanted to reply with something snarky, but I had the feeling it wouldn't be in my best interest.

Thus, I said nothing.

She came closer and closer until we were eye to eye. While she wasn't the size of Rex, she was still pretty large. Think of a Doberman Pinscher on its hind legs and you'll get the idea of it.

"I commend you," she said.

"Thanks," I replied coolly. "So who do I have to fight next to get out of this? All of you?" I swept over the room with my eyes. "I'm hopeful that you'll be honorable enough to at least let me fight you one at a time? Either that, or let me use my crew…" I paused and looked over at them. "Well, maybe not Leland, unless you're going to give him his gun back. He's terrible when it comes to hand-to-hand combat."

"I'm not *that* bad, old chap," Leland argued.

"There will be no further fighting, Mr. Dex," Marissa said. "Again, you've bested our leader."

A revelation struck.

"Wait, wait, wait," I said with a look of concern. "This isn't some deal where *I'm* now your leader, is it?"

The wolves all chuckled in response to that. Even Marissa was grinning in her doggish way.

"No, Mr. Dex," she answered. "You're not a werewolf. You can't be our leader."

I actually already knew that wolves wouldn't let non-wolves run the show, but my head wasn't fully recovered from *Channel* yet and I wasn't given another elixir like I'd received after round one.

That was a relief. It was bad enough dealing with the responsibility of being the chief of the Las Vegas Paranormal Police Department; and I had zero desire to take on a bunch of puppies too.

"So, what's the deal here, then?" I said, motioning to the flock.

"You are to select our next leader, of course," she responded as if I should have known this already.

That *was* a new one to me. I'd never heard of this particular ritual. Then again, I'd never battled for the supreme spot in a werewolf clan either.

I grimaced and then pointed at myself. "Me?"

"It is our way."

"But, uh, I don't know any of you," I said. "I mean, you and I have met…kind of."

"Why does this matter?"

"Do any of you have jobs outside of being werewolves?" I asked the room-at-large. There were nods all around. "Right, and before each of you was hired for those jobs, you had to be interviewed, right?" More nods. "Exactly my point. How could I select one of you to lead the crew without knowing each of your strengths and abilities?"

Marissa nodded slowly. "I see your point, Mr. Dex.

However, you must remember that our ways are different than yours."

That was an understatement. Here we were, standing in the middle of an arena that was housed in the bowels of the Temple Church in London, and I was recovering from a fight with an uberwolf. I didn't have any fellow amalgamites who were just like me. Rex had been the closest I'd ever met, but he was mostly wolf, so that didn't count in this context. If there was another out there who was more like my particular strain of amalgamite, I doubted we would battle each other in order to see who was the alpha of our race. That was something that doggies, dragons, and demons did. Vampires, too, sometimes, but usually they went with cunning and deception as their primary weapons.

"So you want me to judge a fight?" I asked, seeking to clarify what she was looking for from me.

She shrugged. "It's not for me to say how you will choose the leader. I only express that our rituals are different from yours."

What the hell was going on? I wasn't their current leader, but I was somehow responsible for picking the next person to be at the top?

Whatever.

The sooner I chose someone, the sooner I got out of here.

My first inclination was to point at the smallest wolf in the joint in the hopes that he or she would take the pups in a new direction. Then I remembered that the smallest ones tended to be the most vicious. And even if I got lucky and selected a more docile, peace-loving doggie, there'd be challengers lining up before we walked out the door.

"Why me?" I whined desperately.

"Because you removed our leader and you cannot be our leader," Marissa answered. "I thought this would be obvious, Mr. Dex."

"Well, yeah, it is and I knew you'd say that, but I just don't like it, is all." I kind of felt like I was whining at this point. So I took a deep breath and reset myself. "You have to remember that I didn't even want to fight Rex in the first place. That was *your* doing, not mine."

Her eyes flashed. "*I* had nothing to do with that bout, Mr. Dex."

"I don't mean you specifically, Marissa," I assured her, "I meant the wolves of this court in general."

"Ah."

She was the most obvious candidate for the job. This was clear since all the other wolves were already deferring to her at the moment, and since it was obvious that Rex had selected her as second-in-command in the first place.

"Fine," I announced, stepping past Marissa, "I will select from among you, but in order to do so I must first see you all in your human forms."

"Why would you require this?" Marissa asked from behind me. "Our wolf forms are far more telling of our prowess, Mr. Dex."

I glanced over my shoulder at her.

"Were I a wolf and could read other wolves the way you can, I would agree. But I'm not, as you've already pointed out, and therefore cannot judge leadership quality solely how how you all look."

This would certainly have been the perfect time to make another dog-show joke.

I didn't.

"But—"

"Marissa," I barked, something I knew they'd understand, "it is *my* responsibility to choose the next leader, correct?"

"Well...yes."

"Then I will do it my way," I stated with such finality that she had no choice but to acquiesce.

"As you wish," she said, bowing her head slightly. Then she turned to the rest of the room and said, "Everyone to human form, now."

It only took a few moments for the transition to complete, but I have to say that their human forms were a lot less impressive. Well, except for a few of the ladies.

Especially Marissa.

"Well, hello," I said to her with some swagger.

Don't judge me; she was no longer in doggie form here.

She still had the same blond hair and blue eyes, but she was quite a bit more curvy than when in canine mode. The jumpsuit she was wearing hugged those curves nicely, too.

Now, it should be noted that most shifters purchase enchanted clothing, which allowed them to morph without losing their outfits. This industry got set up because the shifter community was sick and tired of having to spend so much money on clothing simply due to rips that occurred when changing from their human form. It was also irritating for them to end up in jail for indecent exposure when they changed back. Another plus to this was that mages and wizards got to use their skills in yet another industry. Actually, it made me wonder if they could enchant my suits to be goop-and-tear resistant.

Also, I'd like to point out that among the supernatural community, it's only considered freaky and taboo for two races to play a game of naughty with each other when they're in their supernatural form. In other words, Marissa as a doggie equals not-on-your-life, brother, but as a human it equals here's-my-hotel-key. Vampires and werewolves tended to avoid each other at all costs, but there had been a few Romeo-and-Juliet moments over the years.

"Unbelievable," I heard the voice of Rachel say behind me. "Seriously, you're just incorrigible."

"Guilty as charged," I replied with a smirk.

Then I reached out and gave her a hug. It was a business-like kind of hug, if that makes any sense. Basically, it was the kind of hug that one friend gives to another. Not a bro-hug, but just your standard run-of-the-mill hug.

It was awkward.

"Okay," she said as I let go. "Thanks for that."

I nodded lamely.

"Look," she said, rolling her eyes, "I don't..." She paused and then blew out a long breath. "Thanks for...this."

"You're my partner, Rachel," I said, and then held up a

finger at Leland, silencing his expected response. "You'd have done the same for me." I looked sideways at her. "Right?"

"Of course, you pumpkin seed."

It was nice to be by her side again, even if only for a little while.

"Mr. Dex," Marissa said, "I hate to interrupt your little reunion, but if you could please select our next leader, we'd like to resume our normal duties, as a matter of course."

She spoke a bit more eloquently in her human form. Actually, it was kind of hot.

"Ugh," said Rachel, clearly knowing what I was thinking. "Seriously, you're impossible."

I shrugged and gave her a mischievous grin.

"I am what I am."

"Yeah, a perv." She crossed her arms. "Not something most people are proud of, you know?"

"I'm not most people," I countered.

"You can say that again."

Okay, so maybe it wasn't great being beside her again. Harvey was annoying, sure, but he wasn't constantly judging me. I knew why she did it, of course, but it was still aggravating.

"Mr. Dex?"

"Yeah, yeah, yeah," I muttered before walking over to study the selection of potential leaders.

CHAPTER 27

I ended up taking a seat in the third row of the arena and spoke with the wolves one by one. It probably wasn't necessary since I was pretty certain that Marissa was going to be the next alpha here, but I figured if I didn't make a show of it, she'd be challenged the moment I walked out the door.

"Name?" I asked as a burly looking fellow approached.

"Steve," he said while wiping his brow with a handkerchief. "Steve Austin."

I glanced up. "Like the astronaut?"

"If you're referring to *The Six Million Dollar Man*," he replied, sounding American, "then yes."

It seemed there were more and more expatriates around these days, especially among the werewolves. It was tough to find an alpha position in the more concentrated areas and some people thought they could hold higher positions by having an accent in a different country. Now, if Steve Austin had been from the South, like Cletus and Merle, it would have been quite funny to see how the British wolves dealt with him.

"It only costs six million dollars to become an astronaut?" I said, not sure what he was talking about.

"Only on a TV show, I suppose," he replied.

"Hmmm." Again, no clue what he was referring to. I just remembered hearing a story about some guy named Steve Austin who was an astronaut in the seventies or eighties. He'd crashed and they rebuilt him with bionic parts and stuff. Maybe that's what cost the six million? Still seemed kind of cheap. "Anyway, what makes you think you should lead this group?"

He cleared his throat and dabbed at his brow again. Obviously he was not ready for a position in command. Cool under pressure was imperative, especially around wolves.

"I'm great with trivia," he started, "I know how to fix pretty much any computer around, and I've been a dungeon master at many AD&D events over the last twenty years."

Harvey coughed the word "nerd."

I glared at him and Rachel punched him on the shoulder.

"Owww," he said.

"All right, Steve Austin," I said and then realized that maybe this was that wrestler guy. Another look at his saggy midsection made me think twice about that possibility. "I've got your information. Next!"

Steve fumbled out of the chair, and up stepped an attractive woman with red hair and brown eyes. She had freckles, too, which I always found cute.

I could feel Rachel's stare on me.

"Uh…name?" I said, going all business.

"Trina," she replied. "Trina Hudson."

"And why do you think you deserve to be the next head of the werewolves, Trina Hudson?"

In response she leaned forward and placed a finger under my chin, pulling my eyes up to meet hers. The stare she was giving me was rather hungry. Not as in she wanted to have my leg for an evening snack, but rather that she wanted to roll around with me in the sack for the evening.

"I don't care about leading the wolves," she said. "I just want to sleep with the man who killed Rex. You have to be something to manage that."

I really didn't want to look at Rachel at that moment.

"Well, I had help, you know," I said lamely.

"You can bring your werebear too."

"Ew," I said reflexively. I had zero interest in bedding down with Harvey in the room, so I said the first thing that came to mind. "Sorry, but uh…he's gay."

Harvey's head shot up so fast that his deerstalker hat nearly flew off his head. Leland gave Harvey an appraising look and nodded.

"What?" croaked Harvey.

"Nothing," Leland stated. "I just wasn't aware of your interest in other fellows. It has absolutely no bearing on anything, of course, I was just surprised."

"I *don't* have an interest in other fellows," Harvey replied through clenched teeth. "He's just saying that to get out of having to bone this chick."

Trina gave me an irritated look. "Is this true?"

"I didn't think he'd hear me," I answered, wincing.

"Asshole." Trina stood up and put her hands on her hips. "At this point, I wouldn't fuck you if you were the last man on Earth."

Then she stormed off.

That stung, and it was kind of embarrassing since everyone else in the room hadn't likely heard the start of her interview.

Rachel was grinning from ear to ear.

"Next!"

After another ten faces and names that had no business even bothering to attempt to be the leader of this pack, I wrapped up my interviews and strode down to the center of the arena.

All eyes were on me as I prepared to announce their fate.

Nobody here really had the wherewithal to run the clan, except for Marissa. Many were strong enough, but they were too ruthless. Others would back down at the first challenge, and some had serious delusions of grandeur. I'd never understood why people tried so hard to become something they weren't, especially when they knew they'd be miserable. Steve Austin, for example, didn't want to be the head of the wolves. He wanted to be their main IT guy. That was it. But he couldn't rightly say that because it'd be considered weak. Once he'd been bypassed in this little ritual, though, he'd…

I glanced up at the thought, wondering how much power I really had here.

Time to find out.

"Okay," I called out, "listen up. I've interviewed all of

you and I have to say that there are some pretty strong candidates in this crowd."

I began pacing back and forth in front of the line of people.

"I'm sure most of you really want a crack at being the top dog, but I also know that you are bound to accept my final decision."

Nobody said a word.

"Before I announce the final person, though, I would like to make a recommendation that Steve Austin be made the head of the IT department for the group."

Steve's eyes lit up, but I could tell he was fighting to play it cool.

There was no argument, so I went on, picking a couple of names from memory that stood out during the interviews.

"I'd also say that Clara Brown should run the weekly combat training systems, with Brett Poole as a second.

I then decided it was time to repay Trina for embarrassing me in front of all of them.

"And Trina Hudson should be in charge of janitorial."

"What?" she shrieked.

I gave her a hard stare. It'd be the only thing hard she'd ever get from me, so I gave it to her good.

The other wolves turned to her.

Obviously, she had breached etiquette with her outburst.

"I mean," she fought to recover, "janitorial has always been a dream of mine."

"That's perfect, then." I left my eyes on hers for

another few moments. "And that brings us to who should be the new leader."

I placed my hands behind my back and surveyed them all. Marissa had to know she'd be the obvious choice, but I nodded at the main candidates a couple of times to make her feel a little less sure of her chances. By the time I had my eyes on her, I could see she wasn't quite as confident as before.

"Now, when I make my selection, I expect everyone to respect my choice. Your rules and regulations make me the arbiter here. Don't forget that."

The air fell still at my proclamation.

"At the same time, I'm going to charge each of you to make sure that your leader does only what is best for the pack, and that means what is best for the community as a whole." All eyes were on me at this point. "If your leader does anything that will bring the law down on your heads, I would wager that I have selected the incorrect person for the job, and I'd hate to have to come back here and set things straight."

Threats. That's how you worked with the wolves. Power and control was what they responded to. Baseless threats did nothing, but they'd seen what I'd done to Rex, so they knew I could back up my statement.

"Are there any questions?"

There were none.

"Good." I then took a few more steps away from them, spun around, and said, "I name Marissa as your next leader."

CHAPTER 28

With the wolves out of my hair, I had to deal with something even more scary: Rachel Cress.

My inner voice was yelling at me to avoid any awkward hugs and to just say "farewell" and get the hell back to Vegas. She'd left to come to London because she needed to do that. It was wrong to argue with her about it, then, and it was wrong to discuss it now.

With that in mind, I said, "We need to talk."

Seriously, sometimes I wondered why I had internal dialog at all.

"I agree," she said, not looking at me as we walked over toward the London PPD HQ that was nestled in a null zone behind the National Gallery gift shop. "Alone."

Hadn't expected that.

"Harvey," I called up ahead as he and Leland prattled on about their various hobbies and such, "why don't you

165

two head back to Leland's headquarters? Rachel and I want to have a talk."

He gave me a wink. "You got it, Chief."

Ugh.

"Ugh," agreed Rachel.

Once we were free of those two, we took a seat on the stairs of the National Gallery. It was a little cold out, but not horribly so. Since it had gotten pretty late, we had a decent level of privacy.

There were tons of fire engines running around and the town was glowing near the bridges and the park.

"What do you think is going on over there?" Rachel asked, pointing.

"Simon Strong and his pal Montague are in town."

"Ah, say no more." She then turned and looked at me. "So, what is it you want to say?"

Yeah, what *did* I want to say? I missed her? I cared about her? I wanted to put Harvey back in charge of the paddy wagon so I didn't have to deal with his oddities?

"I want you back," was all that came out.

"On the Vegas PPD, you mean?"

"No," I answered, "...and yes. Both."

I could tell from the gleam in her eye that she wasn't planning on making this easy.

"I don't understand what you're saying, Ian."

She knew full well what I was saying, but it was no fun for her to just accept that and move on. Honestly, werewolf challenge games were easier than dealing with the likes of Rachel Cress. Yes, wolves hit harder, sometimes, but Rachel dug her nails in. Actually, I kind of liked it when she did that.

I cleared my throat.

"Okay," I said, standing up and walking in front of her and down a few steps. I didn't feel comfortable seated when I was going to say what I was about to say. "These last couple of months have—"

"Wait, wait, wait," she said, her face losing every ounce of mirth. "Please tell me you're not going to get down on a knee, Ian. I'm not ready for that."

"Neither am I," I breathed in horror as my libido passed before my eyes.

She grimaced. "You don't have to act like it's the worst thing imaginable, either. Sheesh."

"Sorry, but both of us are way too young for that level of commitment."

"I'm not," she replied, clearly speaking from the position of maturity.

"Fine, but I am."

I let out a long breath. If we were never going to tie the knot, why should I bother to tell her how I felt? Then again, our kind didn't get married anyway. It just wasn't the way things went.

"Well," I said, building up my courage, "you know what I am. I can't help being that."

"A perv, you mean?"

"Sure," I deadpanned.

"I know you can't help it," she remarked without inflection. "I also know you don't have to flaunt it as much as you do. But you may recall that even when we were together, back in the day, we both continued playing the field."

I blinked at her. "*I* didn't."

"Sure, you did," she said with a laugh. "Remember—"

"No, I didn't."

The blood drained from her face. "Seriously?"

"Yeah. Remember, I'm *very* loyal when I make a commitment, Rachel."

"Huh."

"Apparently, you're not as loyal."

"It's just that I thought we..."

I just shook my head at her as she trailed off.

"And you call *me* a perv."

"You are."

"Seems you're more of one than I am, Rachel."

Her arms uncrossed as mine crossed, signaling that the tables had turned. I wasn't one who got all clingy when I was in a committed relationship, but if I was willing to turn off the hose—uh-hem—then I expected the same in return.

"Sorry," she groaned. "I thought for certain you were playing around, too."

"Yeah, well, I wasn't."

Part of me wanted to keep this angst going on, but that was years ago and this was a new day...or night, anyway. The point was that I wanted her back as my partner, but I also wanted *us* to give things a shot. A real shot. Not a married-level shot, but a real shot nonetheless.

I waved a dismissive hand. "Forget about all that. The fact is that I want you back as both my partner on the Vegas PPD and as my girl."

"Your girl?"

"Don't take that as me being a chauvinist, Rachel. You know I don't mean it that way."

It was apparent that she was fighting to contain her response. At least that was something.

Finally, she glanced away. "Me too," she mumbled.

"What?" I choked out, not sure I'd heard what I thought I heard.

"Me too," she said more loudly, looking up at me. "I want to come back, too." Then she rolled her eyes and added, "And I want to be 'your girl.'" She actually put that last part in hand quotes.

"Seriously?"

She got up and wagged a finger at me. "Don't make me say it again, Ian. I swear I'll kick you in the balls."

I smiled.

"Okay, but we have a few logistical issues to sort out here."

"Leland, Harvey," she rattled off as she headed down the stairs past me, "and the fact that you're the chief and I'm your subordinate."

"Exactly."

We started walking over to the London PPD. I took her hand in mine. It felt odd. Right, but odd. She didn't fight my holding her hand, which was a good sign.

"I can put Harvey back on handling jail pickups for now," I said. "He's been a decent partner, but I never expected it to be permanent. I was just hopeful that you'd eventually come back."

"He'll probably take it hard," she said. "He seems kind of sensitive."

"I know." It was true, too. Harvey would see it as me dumping him. I'd have to let him down easy. "I'll figure it out. Maybe I'll put him with Serena or something."

"Yeah, like *that's* going to go over well."

I laughed. "True."

"As for Leland," Rachel said, "I doubt he'll have any issues with it at all. He's one of those who feels that ladies are meant to fall before him and grovel at his feet."

"Yeah, he does seem to have a James Bond vibe going on." I thought back to a few of the movies I'd seen. "At least Bond respected the level of strength women have."

"Oh, so does Leland," Rachel noted a moment later, "especially after I punched him in the gut when he told me he'd handle all the thinking during our time together."

"Ouch."

"Don't worry, he's changed a lot since Bellows made us partners."

We stopped just inside the null zone before stepping inside.

"As for me being the chief, Rachel, we'll just have to agree that we're all business when on duty. I promise I won't treat you any differently than I do anyone else."

She nodded. "Fair enough. And I promise this time to actually be loyal. Again, I didn't know that you—"

"That's old news," I interrupted. "I'll let it go and so should you."

"Works for me."

"One thing, though..." I said as we walked inside. "How do you feel about valkyries?"

CHAPTER 29

*C*hief Bellows was seated in his office, looking as grumpy as the first time I'd seen him. It made me wonder if the man even remembered how to smile. Looking at him, you'd find it hard to imagine he'd ever even learned how to do it in the first place.

Harvey and Leland were already there when we walked in.

"Good to have you back, Officer Cress," Bellows said in his gruff voice.

"Thank you, Chief," Rachel replied, showing him a level of respect *I* never got.

Bellows then motioned at Harvey and Leland. "Seems we have another problem here, though."

"What's that?" I asked before Rachel could.

"Uh, Chief," Harvey coughed, "I don't want you to take this the wrong way or anything, and I really don't want to hurt your feelings. You've been great. Honestly. Just great." He was shifting around and babbling. "You helped me out of a bad situation with Matilda, and—"

"Who's Matilda?" said Leland.

"My wife," Harvey answered. "She's in prison, though. Long story. I'll tell you later."

"So you're really *not* gay?"

"No, I'm not gay," Harvey said, and then looked at Bellows. "Not that there's anything wrong with being gay."

Bellows' eyes darkened. "Why are you looking at me when saying that? Are you implying something?"

"No, not at all, Chief Bellows." Harvey was clearly beside himself now. "I was just making sure you were clear that I wasn't one of those prejudiced types!"

"Oh, right," Bellows said, coughing.

"Harvey," I coaxed, "get on with what you were saying, will you?"

"It's just that…" He trailed off and then took a deep breath. "It's just that I think it'd be better if I worked with Leland. He and I complement each other's skills really well. I'm a good fighter and he's horrible at it, but he's a great shot and I just don't have a steady enough hand for it."

"I'm not that bad at fighting," Leland argued.

"You're terrible," Rachel stated with a laugh. "Sorry, Leland, but if it weren't for my magic protecting you over these last couple of months, you'd be either in the hospital or the morgue. You're great with a gun, but you couldn't win a fight against a punching bag."

Leland frowned in a pouty way.

"Anyway," Harvey continued, "I'm kind of getting this

feeling like you're going to ask Rachel to come back to the PPD, so…" He must have caught the fact that Rachel and I glanced at each other because he got very smiley. "I knew it! Well, I think that's great, but it leaves me stuck running the bad guys back and forth to the holding cell. That was cool at the start, but now that I've been on the beat for a while, I can't go back to doing that, you know?"

"Yeah," I answered. "I get it."

"So what do you think?"

"It's not up to me, Harvey," I said, tilting my head toward Chief Bellows. "It's his precinct."

Bellows harrumphed and started in on cracking his knuckles. This guy seriously needed some laughing gas or something.

Finally, he looked at me and said, "And I don't suppose you have the room or the budget in the Vegas PPD for these two, right?"

"Sorry, Bellows," I replied truthfully. "I really don't. My jurisdiction is tiny compared to yours."

He grumbled something under his breath as he looked around his desk.

"All right, all right," he said as he pointed sternly at Harvey, "but you're going to treat me with respect, young man. If you ever threaten to shove me into a bin again, I'll have your balls for supper."

I grimaced at that visual. "Why would you want to eat his balls for supper?"

"Agreed," Leland stated with equal disgust. "That's rather disturbing, sir."

"I don't mean it literally, you idiots! It's just…" He paused, his face red as an apple.

"I know what you mean, Chief," Harvey spoke up firmly, "and you've got my word that I won't do anything like that. I only did that before because Chief Dex was my chief at the time...sir."

The implication there was that if Bellows brought Harvey onboard, the werebear would be willing to snap *me* in two and shove me in the trash.

That was a lovely thought.

"All right, then," Chief Bellows said, putting his hands up slightly. "Nobody else wants to work with Leland anyway, so he's all yours."

"That's great," Harvey blurted while doing a mini fist-pump. "And don't worry, Chief," he added as he looked back at me, "if you ever need me for anything, I'll be there for you. Like I said, you helped me out a lot and I owe you for that."

"You don't owe me anything, Harvey," I countered. "You're a good officer." Okay, it was a stretch, but he *did* have potential, and it could just be that Leland was the perfect partner to bring out the best in Harvey. "I'm sure you'll do great."

As for Leland, he just sat there looking confused. "What do you mean nobody else wants to work with me?"

CHAPTER 30

The Vegas squad was elated at seeing that Rachel had returned. Well, everyone but Lydia. She was a bit miffed regarding the fact that Rachel and I were an item again. I assumed that many people would be, truth be told. Dr. Vernon came to mind, and the valkyries, and this particular succubus who had been making a nice wage from working with me for the last couple of months.

"The Directors wish to speak with you, Officer Dex," said Lydia in the same pedantic voice she used with the other officers. "They are waiting."

I shut my office door and sighed.

"Lydia," I spoke in a calm voice, "you know that while Rachel is my girl in the tactile world, you'll always be my digital babe."

"Really?" she said after a moment's hesitation.

"Of course," I answered. "And Rachel knows it too."

She didn't, but I'd tell her in a few weeks, or possibly

175

never. It wasn't like I was going to do the naughty with Lydia or anything and Rachel was well aware of my flirtatious nature. That had never been called into question.

"Well, okay then, sugar plum," she said sweetly. "Honestly, I couldn't have held back anyway. You're just so scrumptious, loverboy."

I cracked a smile. "Thanks, baby."

"You'd better get to your meeting, puddin'."

"Right."

I walked through the door at the back of my office and took the chair that sat before the Directors.

Something seemed off, though. One of the Directors was missing.

"O?" I questioned, trying to peer through the haze. "Is he not here?"

"He's out screwing around with the plot of an author pal of his or something," EQK answered. "Makes no sense to me, but he sure seemed pretty excited about it. Fucking mages."

"Ah, okay."

One of the things that always remained a mystery to me was what mages did in their spare time. I assumed they just sat around reading spell books or something, but it seemed they weren't just relegated to that pastime.

I knew that Rachel, specifically, would be occupied with me until we got into another colossal fight. Let's face it, that was bound to happen. Until then, I'd do my best to keep us going. But when that eventuality did occur, she'd be off doing magely things again. I guess I should ask her to bring me along to one of the events at some point. You know, show a little interest in her profession and such. Beyond just work, I mean.

"We understand that you were able to liberate Officer Cress from her kidnappers," stated Silver.

"Yes, sir." Then, I added, "Officer Smith helped a great deal, too." His strength had, anyway, so I wanted to give him proper credit.

Silver then asked, "He's now part of the London PPD, yes?"

"Correct, and Officer Cress is back on my squad." I thought to bring up the fact that we were dating again, but I decided to let it go. They didn't care what we did as officers as long as it didn't interfere with our work and as long as I treated her the same way I treated everyone else. "I think it's for the best, and so does she."

"Fine," Silver said in an I-don't-really-care voice. "As long as things continue to run efficiently, your crew selections remain yours."

"Yes, sir."

There was a tension in the air. I wasn't sure if it had to do with O being out or something else, but it was pretty apparent. Zack hadn't said anything yet. Maybe he was miffed about something?

"So, Zack," EQK started, as if on cue, "I don't suppose you knew any of the tree-markers who were responsible for kidnapping Officer Cress, do you?"

"Tree-markers?" Zack replied.

"You would rather I said hydrant-markers?"

"I'd rather you not use any derogatory descriptors regarding my people at all, you tiny-winged turd."

Wow. Now that was something you didn't hear from

Zack very often. He was usually the peacemaker of the bunch.

EQK giggled, clearly knowing he'd irked the head of the Vegas Werewolf Pack.

"Did you know some of them, sir?" I ventured.

"I don't have the full list, Mr. Dex," he replied, "but the few names I've seen are familiar to me. They will all be going through a deep reintegration in the Netherworld for their participation in this transgression."

I doubted that was necessary after how I'd left things, but supernaturals hated going through deep reintegration. It was annoying and left you numb for weeks. Standard reintegration wasn't so bad. A day or two of fuzziness was all that came from that, but being put through the deep process…that kind of sucked.

"I think they'll be okay now that the uberwolf is dead, sir," I said, thinking that maybe the rest could just get a standard reintegration. Guys like Steve Austin didn't deserve more than that. "The uber was the one who really caused all of this. The rest were just stuck under his thumb."

"Uberwolf?" Zack coaxed after a moment.

"Yes," agreed Silver, "what are you talking about?"

"Oh, I thought you knew."

"Obviously not, numbnuts," EQK said, "so spill it."

I found that strange at first, but I guess because the uber wasn't in Vegas maybe they didn't know what was going on. I thought they'd all talked or at least had some network of information. Then again, I had that network of information, but I only paid attention to the parts that were under my jurisdiction.

"Right," I said. "Well, the wolf's name was Rex. He was at least a head taller than the rest of them, and he was very strong. It took a couple of my particular skills in order to defeat the guy. Honestly, for a while there I hadn't thought that—"

"You said his name was Rex?" interrupted Zack.

"Yes, sir."

"Did he have any unusual markings, by chance?"

The memory of that *Flashes* event struck, as did the hand-to-hand combat Rex and I had engaged in.

"He had a red circle on his shoulder. Kind of looked like a bullseye."

"Interesting," said Silver slowly.

"That shouldn't be possible," noted EQK without the use of foul language. That made his statement ominous at best. "Seriously, that shit shouldn't be possible."

Okay, so a little foul language, but it was still pretty ominous.

"No," agreed Zack. "It shouldn't."

"Uh, sirs?" I spoke up after a few moments of silence. "Would you mind letting me in on what it is that shouldn't be possible, please?"

"Hmmm? Oh, sorry, Officer Dex." Zack cleared his throat. "This is nothing for you to worry about. That will be all for today. Thank you for your time."

"Wait, what?"

"He said beat it, you cock socket," EQK shouted about two seconds before the Directors faded from view.

I was left seated in a pitch-black room alone, wondering what the hell they had been talking about.

CHAPTER 31

*E*ven though Rachel and I were currently an item, she wasn't a fan of the Three Angry Wives Pub, and she knew that I always went there for a few drinks after finishing a mission.

So, I was on my own.

But this time I wasn't looking to drown my sorrows. This time I was looking for the mysterious vampire known as Gabe.

I walked in and saw him seated at a table near the back of the room. While it was interesting that he was here *every time* I was here, that only spelled that he knew when to expect me. What I never understood was how he knew or why he knew.

"Gabe," I said with a nod as I signaled the waiter to bring me a drink.

"Mr. Dex," he replied in his smooth way. "I trust you are well?"

"Super. How about you? Having a good day?"

"It's been going fine, thank you."

"Business going well?"

He inclined his head slightly. "Business?"

"Well, I don't really know what you do for a living, but I assume there's more to your life than dumping special skills on me and then running off into the night." I squinted. "At least I hope so because that sounds really boring otherwise."

He cracked a smile at that.

"I have many projects that I'm responsible for, Mr. Dex," he answered coyly. "Unfortunately, I'm not at liberty to discuss any of them with you."

"Of course you're not."

The waiter dropped off my usual, a Rusty Nail on the rocks. I gave him a nod and asked for a quick follow-up as I had the feeling this liquid wasn't going to last long. I had no intention of getting drunk, but I certainly needed something to take the edge off.

"I understand that Officer Cress is back with you," he said with an arrogant smirk. I paused my drinking. "Don't be so surprised, Mr. Dex. You're already well aware of the fact that I've been providing you with special skills."

"Too aware," I grunted.

"Surely you're able to make some basic deductions from that fact alone?"

"I am," I replied, "and don't call me Shirley."

I couldn't resist.

"Pardon?"

"Nothing," I answered after finishing the first Rusty Nail of the night. "What I want to know is who you are working for and what's in it for you?"

He took a sip of his Bourbon. At least that's what I assumed it was, based on the color of the liquid.

"As for my employer…" He paused and looked up thoughtfully for a moment. "There is nothing I can share with you regarding that, I'm afraid." He brought his eyes back to mine. "As for what's in it for me, again there is nothing I can share on the subject."

I was feeling a bit more than frustrated with him, but I didn't want to blow up just yet. The fact was that this guy had been giving me some powerful skills. How he'd been managing it, I had zero idea. I'd ask, but what would be the point? He'd just say he couldn't tell me anyway.

"So are you just here to fuck with me?" I said in a defeated tone.

"Mr. Dex," he said, his voice the tsk-tsk type, "I told you when we first met that there would be many ubernaturals coming to attack your city, and I have provided you with various means to battle each of them."

"Without user manuals," I pointed out as another Rusty Nail landed on the table. "I'm slowly getting the hang of it, but would a little help with the basics have killed you?"

His reply was in the way of a sad smile.

As I picked up my second drink, Gabe began scooting out of his chair.

"Leaving already?" I said with a laugh. "Could you at least tell me a bit about Rex? He's already dead, so how could that hurt?" He said nothing, so I pushed forward, hoping for at least *some* nugget of information. "He was an amalgamite like me, right?"

"Not like you, no," he answered.

"But he was an amalgamite?"

"Every ubernatural you've faced has been, Mr. Dex, but none of them are like you." He studied the room uncomfortably. "You're unique."

Was this a case of ask the right questions and maybe get an answer? Could be, but it was also clear that my time with Gabe was up for the night. My pain-in-the-ass crystal ball was clearly anxious to get out of here.

"Seriously, dude, why do you always skedaddle after only a few sentences?"

He began pulling on his black gloves.

"Contrary to what you may think, Mr. Dex," he answered, keeping his voice down, "we are not exactly drinking buddies."

"Actually," I countered, "I'd argue you're the closest thing I've got to a drinking buddy."

He stopped pulling at his gloves and glanced up at me with a raised eyebrow.

"How sad."

I frowned.

"Either way," Gabe continued, "my purpose is to judge your state of mind after each battle and to provide you with what I believe you're going to need in order to combat the next in line."

I pushed up from the table and glared at him.

"Look, pal," I said, taking a risk that he may break if I played it tough, "I've about had enough with all these games. Since the first time we met, you've obviously known something. But you never share it with me." I wanted to wring his neck, but I held myself in check. "You obviously knew all of this crap was going to happen. You showed up after that Chippendale's-looking fucker nearly blew the top off the Excalibur, you gave me that *Flashes* thing to deal with Shitfaced Fred, you gave me *Time* to use against Charlotte, and then I got *Sniff* in order to find Rachel." I held up a finger. "And note that Rex was in London, not Vegas, so it should have been one of the officers there dealing with that shit, not me."

He had his hands behind his back as I faced him. Clearly, he wasn't worried in the least that I might get physical if he didn't talk. Guys like him wouldn't divulge any secrets, even if you threatened to cut off their balls and use them for a game of hacky sack.

"Obviously you know more than you're letting on," I said tightly. "So why the games?"

The look in his eye said he wanted to tell me more about the situation but he couldn't.

"You said you were going to lend me support where you could, Gabe," I pressed, hoping to appeal to his sense of honor, if he had any, "so help me out here, pal."

"I am assisting you greatly, Mr. Dex," he answered as he pulled at his gloves again. "Believe it or not, I am."

We stood staring at each other for a few moments, but I knew this was pointless. He wasn't going to spill the beans.

Bastard.

"Fine," I said, throwing up my hands in disgust. "Well, what's the next magic word you're going to give me that I won't know how to use?"

"*Words*," he replied.

"More than one this time, eh?"

"No," he said slowly. "The word I'm giving you is '*Words*.'"

"Oh," I said as *Words* locked into my brain. "I see. Any hints on how to use it?"

His face betrayed no emotion this time. "Sorry."

"Is there a limit to the number of uses, like I have with *Time*?"

"One."

"One use?"

He nodded and spun on his heel, heading out of the pub, leaving me standing there fuming. The second Rusty Nail disappeared in a flash.

"Use it wisely, Mr. Dex," Gabe called back as the door began to close behind him.

Honestly, I was really starting to hate that guy.

Montague & Strong Detective Agency

So you're probably wondering who Simon Strong and Montague are, right? They were the guys that Ian slammed into outside of McDonald's in the middle of London.

Well, they're the primary characters in a fantastic urban fantasy series called "The Montague & Strong Detective Agency" by Orlando A. Sanchez. The books a full of action, humor, and are just downright fun. In Orlando's latest M&S novel, entitled *Silver Clouds Dirty Sky*, he also recounts how Simon and Monty run into Ian Dex, but it's done from their perspective instead!

∿

Pick up your copy of *Silver Clouds Dirty Sky* on Amazon and be sure to check out the entire Montague & Strong Detective Agency series!

Thanks for Reading

If you enjoyed this book, would you please leave a review at the site you purchased it from? It doesn't have to be a book report… just a line or two would be fantastic and it would really help us out!

John P. Logsdon
www.JohnPLogsdon.com

John was raised in the MD/VA/DC area. Growing up, John had a steady interest in writing stories, playing music, and tinkering with computers. He spent over 20 years working in the video games industry where he acted as designer and producer on many online games. He's written science fiction, fantasy, humor, and even books on game development. While he enjoys writing lighthearted adventures and wacky comedies most, he can't seem to turn down writing darker fiction. John lives with his wife, son, and Chihuahua.

Christopher P. Young

Chris grew up in the Maryland suburbs. He spent the majority of his childhood reading and writing science fiction and learning the craft of storytelling. He worked as a designer and producer in the video games industry for a number of years as well as working in technology and admin services. He enjoys writing both serious and comedic science fiction and fantasy. Chris lives with his wife and an ever-growing population of critters.

CRIMSON MYTH PRESS

Crimson Myth Press offers more books by this author as well as books from a few other hand-picked authors. From science fiction & fantasy to adventure & mystery, we bring the best stories for adults and kids alike.

www.CrimsonMyth.com